THE CELEBRITY DOCTOR'S PROPOSAL

BY
SARAH MORGAN

MILLS & BOON®

First published in Great Britain 2005
Large Print edition 2006
Harlequin Mills & Boon Limited,
Eton House, 18-24 Paradise Road,
Richmond, Surrey TW9 1SR

© Sarah Morgan 2005

ISBN 0 263 18851 5

Set in Times Roman 17 on 19 pt.
17-0106-44458

Printed and bound in Great Britain
by Antony Rowe Ltd, Chippenham, Wiltshire

CHAPTER ONE

'I CAN manage without you just for the summer. I want you to go off and breathe mountain air and forget all about medicine and your patients.' Anna turned off the motorway and followed the signs for the airport. She was all brisk efficiency, mentally ticking off things to be done when she got home. There were lots of them. *Too many.* Her life was manic, but she loved it that way. 'And when you come back your lungs will be better and you'll be totally refreshed and raring to go.'

At least she hoped he would be because she couldn't keep this pace up for much longer.

David McKenna glanced across at her with a tired smile. The smile said it all. 'We both know that that isn't true. The truth is that you should be looking for a new partner. I'm getting too old for this, Anna,' he said gruffly. 'Your dad and I set up the practice almost thirty-five years ago. It's time for new blood.'

'That's right.' His wife, Elizabeth, nodded agreement, a determined look in her clear blue eyes as she leaned forward from the back seat to join in the conversation. 'It's time for us to enjoy retirement and our grandchildren.'

Anna glanced in her rear-view mirror and laughed. 'You don't have any grandchildren.'

'Not yet,' Elizabeth agreed placidly as she settled back in her seat and adjusted her seatbelt. 'But it's going to happen shortly.'

Anna carefully fixed her eyes back on the road and clamped her jaw closed. Safer to do that than voice an opinion on *that* particular subject. The McKennas only had one son and he showed absolutely no inclination to settle down. He was far more interested in pursuing a glamorous career as a high-profile media doctor and dating everyone female.

And he drove her nuts. Always had done. Always would do.

Anna ground her teeth and tightened her grip on the steering-wheel. The mere thought of the man was enough to raise her blood pressure to dangerous levels. Every time she turned on the television, Sam McKenna was on the screen, giving his opinion on something medical. Dr Smooth. Dr Handsome. She doubted he even remembered what it was like to be a real doctor. He'd spent far too long in front of the cameras to remember how to diagnose anything other than an ingrowing toenail.

Reminding herself that dwelling on Sam McKenna wasn't good for her health, she turned her attention back to the present and braked neatly as a car cut in front of her. 'You can't possibly talk about retiring, David,' she said briskly, adjusting her speed to ensure a safe following distance. 'The patients love you and you're a brilliant doctor.

And you know you enjoy it. You just need to get yourself well again.'

The practice needed him. The practice he and her father had built from nothing. *She needed him.* She didn't want her life to change. She liked it just the way it was.

David looked at her thoughtfully. 'It will be interesting to see how you find working with the locum I've arranged,' he said idly. 'We both know you've been carrying the lion's share of work for months now. You might find you prefer a younger person who can share the load fairly.'

Anna shot him a quick glance, her brown eyes searching. There was something in his tone that wasn't quite right. But the look he gave her seemed completely innocent so she decided that she must have imagined it.

'I don't want younger,' she said firmly, flicking the indicator and turning towards the airport. 'I want *you.* With all your experience. Which reminds me—we've been so busy, you still haven't told me anything about this locum. You just arranged it all. I hope he knows something about medicine.'

But she wasn't really worried. She trusted David's judgement in everything. If David thought the locum would cope then she had no doubt that he would.

'Of course he does. And you've been far too busy to bother you with the details,' David said vaguely, glancing at his watch and casting a pointed glance at his wife. 'We don't have time for you to dither in the airport, dear.'

'I never dither,' Elizabeth protested with dignity, and her husband smiled.

'So why are we late?'

Anna glanced at them fondly as she pulled up outside the terminal building. Since her own parents had died, Elizabeth and David had stepped into the role. And why not? David had been at medical school with her father. They'd worked together for all those years and she'd taken over her father's role in the practice when he'd been forced to retire because of ill health. It was hardly surprising that the McKennas regarded her as a daughter.

Suddenly filled with an awful feeling that her whole life was about to change, and hating the thought, Anna switched off the engine and turned towards them. 'I want you to be careful,' she said urgently, undoing her seatbelt and reaching across to hug David. 'I want you to rest and take it easy. I couldn't bear it if anything—' She broke off, a lump in her throat, and David hugged her back, as understanding as ever.

'Nothing's going to happen to me, Anna, so stop worrying,' he said gruffly, stroking her long, dark hair with an affectionate hand. 'It was just a nasty dose of pneumonia brought on by mixing with too many ill patients! I'm recovering well and I'm intending to see my grandchildren grow up.'

Anna sniffed and then gave him a shove. 'You're definitely getting senile. I keep telling you, you haven't *got* any grandchildren.'

'Yet.' Over the top of her head, David winked at his wife. 'Gather your belongings, woman. Time to get this show on the road.'

Anna pulled away from him, feeling as though something momentous was happening. Suddenly she really, really didn't want them to go. Which was utterly ridiculous, she told herself firmly, since this whole sabbatical idea had been her brainchild.

What was the matter with her?

She wasn't the sentimental sort. She was practical and efficient and she really tried not to let emotions get in the way. David and Elizabeth needed a break and it was great that they were finally having one. She should be delighted. It was just the last few months, she decided, stepping out of the car and walking round to retrieve the luggage from the boot. She'd been working too hard. Not having enough time off.

Suddenly she envied David, taking a long break.

She tugged one of the cases from the boot, the reality of her life looming large in her brain. 'David, you still haven't told me about this locum and I—'

'Oh, no!' David peered into the boot and pulled a face. 'Don't say we forgot the green case. Elizabeth, did you remember to bring the green case from the bedroom?'

'It's here.' Anna shifted the luggage. 'Under the blue one.'

She dragged it out and added it to the pile on the pavement.

'Thank goodness for that. It contains all my reading matter.' David rummaged in his pocket for his glasses. 'All right, now, have we got everything? Tickets, passports, money—'

Anna tried again. 'About this locum—'

'Surgery door keys? Did we give Anna the spare set?' Elizabeth fussed in her handbag and Anna realised with a mixture of frustration and affection that neither of them was taking the slightest bit of notice of her. They were already on holiday. Far away from life in a Cornish fishing village. Far away from her and the practice.

David patted his other pocket and smiled. 'I left the spares on the kitchen table. Now, we really need to dash.' He leaned forward and kissed Anna on the cheek. 'No need to come in with us. It was wonderful of you to bring us this far. I hate goodbyes and you have to get back to the needy.'

He waved a hand at a porter, who immediately brought a trolley and loaded the bags.

It was only after the glass doors of the terminal building had closed behind them that Anna realised that he'd left without answering her question about the locum.

She gave a sigh of exasperation and settled herself back in the car, ready for the long drive back to Cornwall. She knew nothing about the doctor David had appointed to cover his absence, except that it was a man. But perhaps it didn't matter. She didn't really need to know the details. Just that he was going to turn up.

Knowing that the summer holidays were almost upon them, Anna just hoped he liked hard work. Because he was going to get it in spades.

'Do you think she's guessed?' From inside the privacy of the terminal building, David watched Anna's little car pull away. 'She kept asking and I kept evading the question. Now she thinks I'm going senile.'

'She was joking. If she'd guessed then we wouldn't be standing here now,' Elizabeth said calmly. 'You know what our Anna is like when she loses her temper. We'd be lying in pieces on the pavement and the fire brigade would be on their way.'

David rubbed a hand over the back of his neck and cast her a dubious look. 'I hope we've done the right thing. Just because you and Anna's mother always had this thing about our children marrying each other…'

'You and Philip had the same dream,' Elizabeth reminded him firmly, 'and don't think Susan and I didn't know it. You wanted to hand the practice over to the two of them. You still do.'

Her husband shot her an impatient look. 'Well, of course I do. It would be perfect. The only thing that isn't perfect is that they can't stand the sight of one another. I have to admit that, much as I would like this whole plan to work, I can't see how it is going to.'

Elizabeth delved into her handbag for a mirror. 'They're both strong characters. Neither would want an insipid partner for the journey through life. They suit each other. It's just that they're both too stubborn and blind to see it themselves and that's just because they've never been forced to spend time together. Hopefully, by the time we return, they'll have discovered that they can't live without each other.'

David pulled a face. 'They might kill each other first.'

'Possibly.' Elizabeth gave a womanly smile and checked her lipstick. 'But I don't think so. Now, that's our flight they're calling. Are you ready?'

David cast a glance through the window again but Anna's car was long gone. 'There are going to be fireworks in Cornwall tonight,' he muttered, and his wife clipped her bag shut and gave him a little push.

'Then it's just as well we'll be in Switzerland. Now, stop worrying. Everything is in place and we can do no more. We have to leave the rest up to fate and the chemistry that has always been there between those two. Oh...' She gave a smug smile. 'And then there's the whole of the village, of course. I'm sure they'll be only too happy to give fate a helping hand.'

Anna drove home, mentally listing all the urgent jobs that had to be done. *Too many jobs, not enough time.*

She just hoped the locum was a good swimmer because he was going to be thrown right in the deep end with no buoyancy aid.

The sun blazed down on the car, the sea sparkled and Anna turned up the volume on the radio. Cornwall in the summer might be a crazy place to work but it was a beautiful place and she'd never want to live anywhere else. She smiled and the smile lasted for the time it took for her to pull up outside the surgery.

She was met by a film crew and her smile went out like a light.

For a moment she just sat in her little car and stared at the big van and the cameras and then finally she opened the door and ventured outside.

'Are you Dr Riggs?' A man with a microphone scurried over to her and she nodded.

'Yes. Is there a problem? What's going on here?'

'Just hold it right there.' The man held up a hand to halt her movement and gestured to the cameraman. 'We want to get some footage of you greeting Dr McKenna. Wait just a moment...'

Footage? Of her greeting Dr McKenna?

To the best of her knowledge, she'd just waved Dr McKenna off at the airport and there was only one other Dr McKenna that she knew of, and he wasn't...

She glanced at the film crew again and shook her head in denial.

Oh, no. No. No. David wouldn't have done that to her. He couldn't...

Ignoring the man's plea for her to stay put while they prepared to shoot, she slammed her car door and stalked across the small car park towards the group of people gathered by the entrance, a suspicion growing inside her.

'McKenna?' She growled his name like a threat and the people moved to one side. But she had eyes only for one person.

Cool blue eyes swept over her and his mouth tilted slightly. 'Riggs. What an unexpected pleasure.'

He was as handsome as the devil and his arrogance drove her nuts.

'Unexpected?' She slammed her hands on her hips and glared at him. 'This is *my* surgery, McKenna, so how can my presence here be unexpected? What *is* unexpected is the fact that *you're* standing outside it. You'd better have a damn good reason for causing a disturbance.'

He lifted a dark eyebrow in that lazy, careless way that always drove her mad. 'Nice to see you haven't changed. I have to confess that I thought you'd leg it once my father told you that I was coming,' he drawled. 'Never thought you'd show up to greet me. I'm flattered, Riggs. And touched. I obviously mean more to you than I thought.'

'Greet you? I'm not greeting you, and you need to move yourself and that van...' she stabbed a finger towards the offending vehicle, her dark hair swinging over her shoulders as she turned her head '...from my car park before I have it towed away. I have a surgery starting in an hour and at the moment there is no room for my patients.'

'*Our* patients,' he corrected her mildly, not moving an inch, 'and you're going to have to learn not to swear while the cameras are here. You'd be amazed how little it takes to get complaints from viewers. They like their doctors wholesome and clean-living. No sex or swearing.'

She opened her mouth to make a sharp observation about his reputation for the former and then stopped herself. It wasn't worth it. She really didn't care about his sex life. And anyway, something he'd said was jarring inside her head.

She stared at him, drew breath and finally mentally reran the last few sentences. 'Hold on.' She lifted a hand as if to ward him off. 'What did you mean when you said that your dad should have told me you were coming? Tell me he didn't know you were coming. Tell me this isn't what I think it is.'

Surely David wouldn't have done that to her.

He couldn't...

Sam leaned impossibly broad shoulders against the wall and looked at her, a trace of amusement lighting his blue eyes. 'He's been nagging me for more than three months, Riggs. Finally he resorted to emotional blackmail. ''I need this break, Sam, and if I can't find a decent locum I can't leave poor Anna.'' '

His imitation of his father was so good that if she hadn't been so horrified, Anna would have laughed. Instead she gaped at him. 'Locum? *You're* the locum?' Her voice cracked and all her important bodily functions like breathing and staying upright suddenly seemed threatened. It had to be a joke. 'You have a sick sense of humour, McKenna.'

He shrugged. 'Better a sick sense of humour than no sense of humour at all.' He gave her a meaningful look. 'Now, enough chatting. You can thank me later.' He straightened and waved a hand to the cameraman who was still hovering. 'In the meantime, we have work to do.'

She clenched her fists in her palms. He was implying that she had no sense of humour. He'd always accused her of being too uptight. Of not knowing how to relax. Of planning every detail of her life.

'What I mean is, there is no way your dad would arrange for you to be the locum,' she said, her teeth gritted as she spoke. 'He knows we'd kill each other.'

'That possibility does exist,' Sam agreed, stifling a yawn and moving past her with a loose-limbed stride that betrayed absolutely no sense of urgency. 'However, I reckon that if you stay in your space and I stay in mine, we should just about manage to coexist without significant injury.'

'Wait a minute.' She elbowed her way past the cameraman and planted herself in front of Sam again. Strands of dark hair trailed over her face and she brushed them back with an impatient hand. 'If you're really the locum, why are *they* here?' She glared at the film crew as if they were a disease and he muttered something incomprehensible under his breath.

'They're here because I have a job to do,' he said bluntly. 'Normally I'd be in London, filming a new series. It seems I'm spending the summer in Cornwall so we've had to make some changes to the programme. We've had to adapt. You ought to try it some time.'

At that point, the woman who had been hovering at a tactful distance stepped forward. 'It's going to be brilliant, Dr Riggs.' She reached out and shook Anna's hand. 'I'm Polly. I'm the producer of this series of *Medical Matters*. When Sam told us he was going to be working down here, we decided to do a whole series on summer health. It will be fantastic. We can look at taking care of yourself in the sun, first aid—everything families should know before they go on holiday.'

Warm and friendly, she listed her ideas with enthusiasm, and in normal circumstances Anna would have liked her immediately. But these weren't normal circumstances. And she couldn't like anyone who looked at Sam McKenna with such blatant adoration.

'This is a busy practice,' she said crisply. 'We work flat out to cater to the needs of the locals and at this time of year our numbers double because of the tourist population. We don't have time for film crews.'

'But that's the beauty of it,' Polly said cheerfully, 'Sam already knows the score. He's used to being filmed all the time. There'll be very little intrusion, I can assure you.'

'The patients won't like it.'

'The patients will love it,' Sam predicted dryly, lifting a hand and shielding his eyes from the sun. 'And if they don't, they don't have to take part. They always have the right to refuse to be filmed. But I can tell you now that they won't.'

'We're going to do a variety of different things,' Polly explained eagerly, 'a straight-forward *Medical Matters* from the surgery, which is our usual format, but we're also going to film on location, do some first-aid stuff on the beach—that sort of thing.'

'It sounds as though you've got it all worked out,' Anna said frostily, her eyes on Sam who simply shrugged. 'We need to talk, McKenna. And we need to do it now.'

Polly glanced towards the cameraman who was still hovering. 'Perhaps we should film you discussing it—it might be interesting.'

'Well, unless you want to film something which needs a warning for bad language and violence, I suggest you switch off the camera and go and have a cream tea in the village,' Anna said sweetly, her eyes still blazing into Sam's. 'You and me. Inside. Now.'

Without waiting for the sharp comment that she knew would come, she turned and strode to the front door, unlocking it and letting herself in. Functioning on automatic, she switched off the alarm and picked up the post, aware that he was behind her.

'Don't you have a receptionist any more? What happened to Glenda?' He peered behind the empty reception area with a frown and she gritted her teeth.

She didn't need his comments on the way the surgery ran.

'Glenda is sometimes a bit late,' she muttered, dropping the post behind Reception, ready for Glenda to sort out when she arrived. 'She'll be here in a minute.'

'Late?' He frowned, his expression suddenly thoughtful. 'But she used to be the most punctual person in the world. Really dedicated. Why would Glenda be late?'

Anna bit her lip. She'd asked herself the same question a few times lately and she was steeling herself to address the matter with Glenda. But there was no way she was discussing this with Sam McKenna.

'It's really none of your business,' she said coldly, and he gave a dismissive shrug.

'Fair enough. Just didn't sound much like the Glenda I used to know, that's all.'

'Well, you haven't exactly been spending much time around here lately and people do change,' Anna said tartly.

He ran a hand over his jaw, his expression thoughtful. 'Have you tackled her?'

She gave an impatient sigh. 'No. No, actually, I haven't. If you must know, I haven't had time to breathe or eat in the last few months, let alone sit down and get cosy with the staff.'

His eyes narrowed and his gaze swept her face. 'That bad, huh?'

She gritted her teeth again and cursed herself for showing emotion in front of Sam. He would waste no time throwing it back at her. 'Not bad. Just busy. And if it's all right by you, I'd like to drop the subject now. When I need your advice, I'll ask for it.'

'No, you wouldn't.' He hooked his fingers into the pockets of his jeans and lounged against the reception desk. He had a lean, athletic physique, honed to perfection by his obsession with dangerous sports. 'You wouldn't ask my advice if you were hanging off a cliff by your fingernails. You're so crazily independent, Riggs, that you'd drown rather than ask someone to throw you a lifebelt.'

'Then it's a good job I'm not drowning,' she said coldly, walking through to the reception area and automatically picking up some scattered toys and returning them to the basket. 'And for your information, I'd take the lifebelt as long as you weren't the one throwing it. Now, are we going to sort this problem out?'

He shrugged and stifled a yawn. 'What's there to sort out? You need a locum. I'm here.'

She straightened one of the chairs. 'As far as I'm concerned, those two statements are not linked.'

He drew a breath and she lifted a hand to indicate that she hadn't finished. 'What I need, McKenna, is a serious doctor willing to do some serious work. What I *don't* need is some image-hungry film-star medic with an over-inflated ego which is going to get in my way every time I try and see a patient.'

To her surprise and immense irritation, he smiled. An all-male, sexy smile that tugged something deep in her pelvis.

Damn, he irritated her.

Completely aware of that fact, he straightened up and strolled towards her, a dangerous gleam in his blue eyes as they swept her face. 'Oh, boy, oh, boy, I really do unsettle you, don't I, Riggs? Why is that, I wonder?'

'Do you want a list?' She backed away, trying to maintain her personal space. 'And I can't imagine this is exactly your idea of heaven either. Why did you agree to it?'

His blue eyes glittered. 'I told you. Emotional blackmail on the part of my father. He was ill. He needed a holiday. He couldn't find anyone else. That kind of thing. Tugs at the heart.'

'You don't have a heart.'

He grinned. 'Ouch. Been reading my press cuttings again, Riggs?'

'Hardly.' Her glance was impatient. 'The way you run your love life—or should I say sex life—is your business. But the practice is my business. Your dad certainly never mentioned to me that he was having trouble finding anyone.'

Sam gave a careless shrug. 'Well, the fact is I'm here now. Make the most of me.'

She angled her head and lifted an eyebrow. 'Excuse me? I'm supposed to be honoured that you've graced us with your presence? Let me tell you something, Dr Charm, I'm not at all convinced you'll know a real patient when you see one. You see, here in real life surgery land, the problems aren't staged.'

His gaze didn't flicker. 'Is that so?'

'What happens when you deal with something that doesn't make good television? Are you going to pass them through to me? Or do you grab a textbook?'

He examined his fingernails thoughtfully. 'You really aren't going to make this easy, are you, Riggs?'

She bit her lip. Somehow he made her feel small, childish. 'It's just that this practice is busy,' she said wearily, sweeping her dark hair away from her face and risking eye contact. 'I need proper help. Heavy-duty help.'

Sharp blue eyes searched hers. 'My dad hasn't been pulling his weight, has he?'

She didn't trust herself not to give too much away so her own eyes slid from his, away from that penetrating gaze that saw too much. 'Your dad is a good doctor. The best.'

'But he hasn't got the stamina that he used to,' Sam said softly, running a hand over the back of his neck and giving a frustrated sigh. 'Damn. It's hard, watching your parents grow older. You have this vision of how they are and you never want it to change. I always knew this moment would come, but that doesn't make it any easier.'

She frowned. 'What moment?'

His hand dropped to his side and his glance was ironic. 'The moment when I have to decide whether to go into the family business.'

'You mean, take your father's place?' She stared at him in horror. 'You can't possibly be serious! You don't need me to remind you that you couldn't wait to leave Cornwall at the earliest opportunity. Even if we go along with your dad's plan, it's only short term. No one suggested it was for ever. He's coming back…'

Sam looked at her. 'And when he does, he'll retire and spend his days fishing.'

Anna shook her head. 'He won't retire.'

Sam gave a sigh and stabbed long fingers through his dark hair. 'He has to. We both know that. And you being stubborn about it isn't going to change that fact.' He paced over to the reception area. 'But while he's working out how to break the news to you that this is all too much for him and he doesn't want to do it any more, we'll get the place in order. And work out a plan. Things are going to have to change around here.'

Anna felt as though she'd been doused in cold water.

She didn't want things to change. She loved the way the practice was now. She loved working with David. They understood each other.

Was Sam right? Was David really planning to tell her that he was going to retire from the practice?

She sank onto the nearest chair, her legs suddenly wobbly. It was a moment before she realised that Sam was pressing a glass of water into her hand.

'Drink something,' he said roughly. 'You've obviously been working too hard. You look done in. You're pale and you've got black rings under your eyes. You always were too stubborn to ask for help. I'm going to get rid of the film crew for now and then come back and we can work out what's to be done.'

Anna took a sip of water and found her voice. 'Whatever's to be done,' she muttered, 'I really, *really* don't want to do it with you, McKenna.'

He was the last person in the world that she could imagine developing a good working relationship with.

He laughed and rose to his feet in a fluid movement. 'Likewise. But seeing as that is what fate has decreed, I'd say we're both in for an interesting summer. Looks like we're going to be meeting at dawn. Swords or pistols?'

CHAPTER TWO

SHE hadn't changed a bit.

Sam strode out of the reception area and paused in the foyer, trying to get his emotions back under control before he faced the camera crew. Anna Riggs always did that to him. Drove him so mad that he needed to pump iron for a week in order to burn off the frustration coursing around his body. Thanks to some nifty avoidance tactics on both their parts, they hadn't seen each other for a couple of years, but she was still the same hard-nosed, bossy control freak she'd always been. Not at all his kind of woman. He liked his women soft and gentle. Anna Riggs was about as soft as steel. And the fact that she had a pair of legs that stopped a man in his tracks didn't do anything to change his opinion of her.

And he'd allowed himself to be manipulated into spending the summer with her.

He smashed a fist against the wall and inhaled deeply. Damn, she was right. They were going to kill each other. What had his father been thinking of, arranging for them to work together when he knew that there was so much animosity between them? When he knew that they were just *so* different? It was all very well saying that they didn't need to see much of each other, but they were running a small practice. They were the only two doctors. How could they *not* see each other?

And how was he going to cope with Anna being confrontational and prickly with a camera stuck in his face all day?

He gritted his teeth and applied his brain to the problem.

The first thing was that the cameras certainly couldn't be allowed free access, otherwise they could find themselves filming bloodshed. He'd have to stage each shoot carefully, making sure that Anna wasn't within firing distance.

And the second thing was that he was going to work as independently as possible. Surely he could just see his patients and she could see hers? Did they really need to talk much?

And he wasn't going to involve himself in the practice. He was going to do the job and then see what happened. And if his father decided to retire, he'd find him the best possible replacement. And it wasn't going to be him. Hadn't his parents always accepted that this wasn't the practice for him? His life was in London. He'd chosen a different path. He didn't want to work here permanently any more than Anna wanted him to.

Satisfied that, given sufficient thought, it would be possible to minimise the contact between them, he finally pushed open the glass door of the surgery and walked into the car park.

*   *   *

Glenda turned up, breathless and apologetic, five minutes before surgery started. She dropped her bag behind the reception desk and smoothed her hair, clearly flustered.

'Are you OK?' Anna frowned in concern and Glenda gave a bright smile.

'I'm fine. Sorry I'm a bit late. I was caught up.'

Caught up with what? Anna wanted to ask, but now wasn't the time with a busy surgery about to start and Sam strolling across the reception area as if he'd worked here all his life.

How could he be so relaxed?

'Hi, Glenda.' He gave the receptionist a big hug and for some reason that she couldn't quite identify Anna felt her tension rise.

It was just her that he needled and goaded. With everyone else he was capable of being extremely civilised. Warm. People in the village had always adored Sam McKenna and now he was a major TV personality they never stopped talking about him.

Glenda's face softened. 'Oh— Dr McKenna. How lovely to see you.' She pulled away and tried to straighten her hair, her movements jerky and uncoordinated. 'I suppose you'll be helping our Anna. Good thing, too. She needs some help around here. She's been struggling for far too long.'

Anna's frown deepened. Glenda knew that she and Sam didn't see eye to eye on anything. Why would she think it was a good thing that he'd arrived? Had she known that David had appointed him as locum?

Or was it just that she wasn't concentrating because she had something else on her mind?

She hated to admit that Sam was right about anything, but suddenly Anna decided that a conversation with the receptionist was becoming a priority.

'Busy surgery.' Glenda flicked on the computer and checked the appointments, seeming more flustered than usual. 'Open those doors and let the battle commence.'

Resolving to tackle Glenda in private later, Anna turned to Sam. 'I know that this is throwing you in at the deep end, but can you take your father's surgery? I expect you'll know some of the patients anyway, and if you need to know anything that isn't in the notes you can buzz through to me. Press 4 on your phone. Or I'm just next door.'

Sam lifted an eyebrow, his expression mocking. 'Sure you don't want to sit in with me, just to be sure that I don't kill anyone?'

She gritted her teeth. 'I don't think you're about to kill anyone.'

'No.' His voice was dry. 'You just think my clinical skills are rustier than an old garden fork.'

'I'm just aware that it's probably a long time since you did a consultation that wasn't staged. The way our surgeries run at the moment, there's not a lot of time to look in a textbook between cases. And you only get the one take.' Anna sucked in a breath. 'I was *trying* to be helpful. Next time I won't bother.'

'Good idea. You worry about your own patients. I'll worry about mine.' Without giving her time to respond, Sam strode down the corridor towards his father's consulting room.

'I'm going to kill him.' For the first time since she was five years old, Anna found herself wanting to stamp her foot. With an enormous effort of will she managed to restrict herself to an inward growl of frustration. 'Well, at least we don't need to change the name on his door,' she muttered, and then turned to Glenda who was watching open-mouthed. 'Don't look like that.'

Glenda found her voice. 'Nice to see that neither of you have changed,' she said faintly, and Anna sighed.

'Oh, don't make me feel guilty. Maybe I shouldn't have spoken to him like that, but the guy drives me crazy. And whatever he says to the contrary, he hasn't seen a real patient for ages. Diseases that they stage for the camera aren't the same thing at all.'

Glenda frowned. 'Anna, I thought he'd—'

'He won't admit it, of course, because he's a man, and a man with a big ego,' Anna said, reaching forward to pick up a pile of results, 'but you'd better keep an eye on him, Glenda. If you think he's got a problem with someone, let me know because his pride won't let him do it himself and he certainly won't ask me.'

Glenda looked confused. 'But, Anna, I thought that Dr McKenna—'

'Oh, let's drop the subject for now,' Anna muttered, deciding that she'd had enough of talking about Sam McKenna. 'Just buzz me if you think there's a problem.'

With that, she walked through to her own surgery and settled herself behind her desk. Instantly she felt calmer and more in control. This was her space, a place that she loved, and even having Sam next door couldn't spoil it.

She switched on her computer and pressed the buzzer for her first patient. Seconds later there was a tap on the door and a young mother entered, struggling with a wriggling toddler.

'Hello, Heather, how are things?' Anna had been in the year above Heather at school and the two of them were still friends.

That was the wonderful thing about general practice, she mused as she stood up and walked around her desk to admire the baby. You knew the patients. Not like Accident and Emergency where she'd spent six months during her GP rotational training. There the patients were little more than cases and numbers. In general practice the patients had lives. They were real. And the family doctor was part of all that. It was a job worth doing.

'It isn't me, Anna,' Heather murmured, settling herself in the chair and trying to persuade the whining toddler to sit still with her. 'It's Grace. She's had a personality change lately and, frankly, I'm ready to scream.'

Anna reached for her favourite puppet and slipped her hand inside. 'Hi, Grace,' she said cheerfully, waggling the furry fox at the toddler. 'Nice of you to visit me.'

The little girl stopped grizzling at once and stared at the puppet, transfixed. Then she held out a hand to stroke its nose. 'Fox.'

'That's right.' Anna waggled the puppet. 'Fox.' While the little girl's attention was caught she questioned the mother. 'So what's been happening, Heather?'

'It's Grace. She just doesn't seem to listen to me any more,' the young mother said helplessly. 'She takes absolutely no notice of anything I say and she's so loud all of a sudden. She shouts all the time.'

Anna frowned. 'How long has it been going on for?'

'I don't know.' Heather shrugged. 'A couple of months, I suppose. We had a terrible winter with her as you know. We virtually lived in your surgery with colds.'

Anna tickled Grace's ear with the puppet and reached across her desk for some equipment. 'How's her speech?'

'Well, she was doing really well but if anything she's slipped back.' Heather gave a rueful smile and cuddled the little girl closer. 'Whoever said being a mother was easy? Do you think it's just her age? That she's just being naughty?'

'No, I don't. I suspect that she might have glue ear,' Anna said calmly, judging whether it was a good moment to abandon the fox in favour of a clinical examination. 'Heather, hold out your hand. I need you to take over acting duties while I take a look at her ears.'

Heather dutifully slipped her hand inside the puppet, leaving Anna to concentrate on the little girl.

'Grace, I'm just going to look inside the fox's ears,' she said cheerfully, 'and then I'm going to look inside yours.'

Grace watched with round eyes as Anna pretended to look inside the puppet's ears, then she sat still while Anna gently used the auriscope to examine her.

'I'm just checking that there's no wax or foreign bodies,' she murmured as she examined the eardrum. 'Oh, yes, there's the problem. I see it. The eardrum is very dull and looks indrawn. She definitely has glue ear.'

'Glue ear?' Heather frowned. 'What exactly is that?'

'It's a condition where the child has fluid deep in the ear,' Anna explained, 'but without signs of infection. It's called glue ear because the fluid tends to be like runny glue— thick, clear and sticky.'

Heather pulled a face. 'Sounds awful. But why does that make her shout?'

'Because I suspect it is affecting her hearing.' Anna reached for a pad and scribbled a simple diagram. 'People can hear because sound waves are transmitted via their eardrums and tiny bones inside the middle ear. The eardrum and bones vibrate.'

Heather stared at the diagram and pulled a face. 'I was always bottom in biology.'

Anna smiled and put the pencil down. 'Doesn't matter. All you need to know is that in glue ear the middle ear, which is usually full of air, becomes filled with a sticky fluid and that damps down the vibrations.'

'And stops the child from hearing?'

'It can do.' Anna stood up. 'It's very common in children so don't think Grace is the only one. Speech is affected because she isn't hearing well.'

'So what do we do about it?'

'Fortunately glue ear almost always settles down of its own accord but if Grace's hearing gets worse then we may need to look at referring her to an ENT specialist. But at the moment I don't think we should do that. I'm going to refer her to the audiology department for an assessment of her hearing and we'll take it from there.'

'So she doesn't need antibiotics or anything now?'

Anna shook her head. 'She doesn't have an infection so they won't work. I'm fairly confident that if we leave it alone it will go by itself, but we'll keep a close eye on it and if we're worried at any point then we can refer her.'

'I'm not wild about her having an operation,' Heather admitted, and Anna smiled sympathetically.

'I doubt it will be necessary so let's cross that bridge when we come to it. I'll refer her to Audiology today and you'll get a letter from them in the next month or so, inviting Grace to come for a test.'

'Thanks, Anna.' Heather stood up and brushed her curls away from her face, her cheeks slightly pink. 'I heard a rumour that our Sam's back. Is it true that he's going to be working here for the summer?'

Anna stiffened. Not if she could find a way out of it. 'Well, he's here at the moment, but he may not be able to stay for the whole summer.'

At least, not if she had anything to do with it.

'Oh, I hope he can,' Heather enthused, shifting the toddler more comfortably in her arms. 'I mean, it's so brilliant having him. I never miss him on the telly. He's so sympathetic, isn't he? So warm. Can't believe it's our Sam, really.'

Our Sam.

Anna clamped her jaws together and resisted the temptation to point out that Sam McKenna was a gifted actor and was warm when it suited him to appear that way. With her he was about as warm as the polar ice-pack.

Then she remembered that Heather had had a massive crush on Sam when they'd been at school. As had most of the girls. Except her.

Anna rolled her eyes. She and Sam had been thrown together a lot because of their parents' working relationship and at one time she knew that both sets of parents had harboured a fond hope that they might take over the practice. But that had never been an option for Sam. He hadn't been able to wait to get away.

And just as well, she thought briskly, otherwise there would have been bloodshed. She and Sam would *not* have made a good partnership. They clashed on just about everything.

Heather was still talking. 'Everyone thinks it would be great if he stayed permanently,' she gossiped happily. 'I mean, it used to be both your dads, then it was you and his dad and now it could be the two of you.'

'I don't think so.' Anna rose to her feet so rapidly she almost knocked the chair over. Aware that Heather was looking at her in surprise, Anna produced a smile. 'You're jumping the gun, Heather. This is temporary. Just temporary.'

And she certainly didn't want that sort of gossip and speculation spreading around the village.

'Well, you never really know how things are going to turn out, do you?' Heather said sagely, standing up and reaching for her bag. 'Thanks, Anna. See you soon.'

She left the surgery and Anna stared after her. Heather had said, *Everyone thinks.* So did that mean that everyone in the village were already aware that Sam was here? Did that mean that the whole village already thought that this might be a permanent arrangement?

No, no, no.

She covered her face with her hands and stifled a groan. If it turned out to be a permanent arrangement then she would have to leave. There was no *way* she could spend every day working alongside Sam. Her blood pressure wouldn't be able to stand it.

But he wouldn't stay, she consoled herself, applying logic to the situation. No way. Sam had chosen a very different life for himself. The City. Bright lights. Fame and fortune. He wouldn't last five minutes in a sleepy Cornish fishing village. In fact, she doubted he'd even last the summer. He'd already made it clear that there wasn't enough here to keep him entertained.

Cheered by that thought, she buzzed for her next patient and steadily worked her way through her afternoon list.

When she finally emerged from her surgery, she found Glenda deep in conversation with Sam who was perched on the desk, an intent expression on his handsome face.

Glenda coloured and broke off the moment she saw Anna, and Sam slid off the desk and walked towards her.

'So, how did your surgery go, Riggs? Nothing you needed to ask me about?'

She ignored his sarcastic tone and gave him a withering look. 'When I need help, I'll consult a textbook.'

'How boring,' he drawled, lifting a hand and tucking a strand of her long dark hair behind her ear. 'Better watch it, the country girl is trying to escape.'

Country girl.

It was what he'd always called her when she'd been little. He'd loved to tease her for being so at home in the outdoors. Unlike him, she'd never been comfortable with bright lights and hordes of people.

Aware that his fingers were still in her hair, she jerked her head away from him with a frosty glare, handed Glenda a pile of results for filing and stalked back to her room. For a moment she just stood there, sucking in deep breaths, and then she moved over to the wash-basin and opened the taps, splashing her face with cold water to cool her burning cheeks.

'Drowning yourself?'

She reached for the towel, dried her face and turned slowly. 'Just answer me that one question, McKenna. Why? Why did you come here? We both know that a GP practice in Cornwall isn't where you see your future. So why are you here? Or have they run out of women in London?'

He strolled into the room and leaned narrow hips against her desk, wickedly handsome and altogether too dangerous for words. 'You know the answer to that. I'm here because Dad asked me to come. And because Cornwall isn't a bad place in the summer.'

He was winding her up and she knew it. Even he couldn't fail to like Cornwall in the summer. Especially as being here would undoubtedly allow him to indulge in his favourite sports. She knew he'd be kite-surfing and windsurfing the moment he'd unpacked his suitcase.

'So this is a free holiday.' She ground her teeth. 'You could have said no. You *should* have said no.'

He raised a dark eyebrow. 'Why?'

'Because you know this isn't going to work, that's why.'

'I hate to disappoint you but saying no to a sick man, especially when that sick man is my father, isn't exactly my forte.' He gazed at one of the photographs on her wall and

Anna bit her lip, hating the intrusion into her personal space. 'That's nice. Bedruthan steps. Do you remember that time we were almost cut off by the tide? You always loved that beach when we were kids.'

'Stop changing the subject. You could have pretended you couldn't get away. You could have encouraged him to arrange a locum.'

'He did arrange a locum. Me.' Sam ran a hand over the back of his neck and shot her an impatient look. 'All right, you tell me how I was supposed to say no. With Dad so ill and Mum so worried, how was I supposed to say no?'

'You've said no before, lots of times.'

'When he's asked me to join the practice, to be part of the family firm,' Sam agreed. 'This is different. This is an emergency. I don't say no to emergencies.'

'Just to commitment.' The words were out before she could stop them and even before she saw the narrowing of his eyes she regretted them. 'Forget I said that. The way you run your life is none of my business.'

'No, it isn't.' He folded his arms across his chest, his gaze fixed on hers. 'But the way I run my life clearly bothers you.'

Suddenly the room felt unusually warm. 'It doesn't bother me. What bothers me is that you're going to swan in here for a few weeks or until you get bored then leave us in the lurch.'

'No, that isn't what bothers you.' His gaze didn't shift. 'What really bothers you is the fact that you haven't planned this and we both know that you have to plan everything. You think you have your whole life sorted, don't you, Riggs?'

'There's nothing wrong with planning.' She wondered why she was defending herself to someone she didn't even like.

'Except that life has a way of throwing you surprises. And it's harder to cope with surprises if you're inflexible.'

'I'm not inflexible. And you're not a surprise, McKenna. You're a nightmare.'

'I promised my father I'd stay for the summer and that's what I intend to do.'

'Along with your film crew.'

He shrugged. 'Life goes on. When I return to London in the autumn I'll want to pick up where I left off. The film crew is part of my life.'

Anna shook her head. 'It isn't going to work, McKenna.'

'It'll work if you don't get all high and mighty on me. Why shouldn't it?' He was as direct as she was, hard and uncompromising in his approach to life. 'Because I'm the only person you can't control, Riggs? Because I don't fit your image of a doctor? Because I don't do things the way you do them?'

She tilted her head, her gaze cool. 'Because you drive me nuts.'

'Likewise.'

Their eyes locked in combat for endless minutes and then she gave a sigh. 'All right.

Let's look at the facts here. I need help and I don't have time to look for a new locum. You're here. You can stay until I find a suitable replacement. But there are rules.'

'You amaze me.' He folded his arms across his broad chest. 'And there I was thinking you were such a relaxed, laid-back person. Always willing to go with the flow.'

She chose to ignore his sarcasm. 'No filming without my permission, and the patients' permission, and if it interferes with your workload then it stops.'

His eyes glittered dangerously. 'Anything else?'

'Yes, actually.' Her tone was businesslike with just a touch of frost around the edges. 'I'm the partner in this practice, you're the locum. You do things my way. If you disagree, we still do things my way.'

'What if my way's better?'

She gritted her teeth. He was doing it on purpose, of course. Annoying her. Irritating her. Winding her up so tightly that she was ready to explode. 'It won't be. You don't have any experience of primary care. And even if you did, why would you even care about changing things? We both know you won't be hanging around long enough to make an impact.'

He studied her carefully. 'Unfortunately, Riggs, your rules don't work for me. If I see something that I think needs changing I'm going to say so and we're going to talk about it. I may be the locum but I still have an opinion on how the practice is run and you're going to listen to it. Starting with Glenda.'

Anna stared at him. 'What about Glenda?'

'What do you know about her home life?'

Anna frowned, thrown by the sudden shift in the conversation. 'Well, I know she lives with her elderly mother in a cottage down by the harbour. Her mother is your father's patient and to be honest I haven't seen much of her for the past few years so I can't honestly say I know her. She doesn't go out much. Why?'

'Because her mother is the reason Glenda was late this morning. She had her buttons done up in the wrong holes,' Sam said calmly. 'She hasn't told me much yet but she hinted that her mother isn't herself.'

'I didn't know that. Your father hasn't said anything.' Anna felt a twinge of guilt that she hadn't found the time to question Glenda's lateness herself. If she was honest, she'd found it more annoying than concerning. It hadn't occurred to her that something might be wrong. She bit her lip. She was the doctor, for goodness' sake. She should have noticed that Glenda was upset about something.

It annoyed her that Sam had spotted it first and it made her feel guilty.

Resolving to talk to the receptionist immediately, Anna poured herself a glass of water and took a few sips.

'This practice is stretched to the limit,' Sam said grimly, 'and we need efficient staff. If Glenda can't perform the role then we need to get someone in who can.'

Anna slammed the glass down on the table. 'And what are you proposing to do with Glenda?' Her eyes sparked into his. 'Fire her?'

'No, actually.' He stood in the centre of her consulting room, legs planted firmly apart, totally comfortable and maddeningly sure of himself. 'Support her. And expecting her to fulfil a full-time employment commitment with what I suspect is a major family problem brewing isn't support.'

Anna sagged slightly, her conscience pricking her. 'Oh, hell. You're right,' she muttered, rubbing her fingers across her temples to ease the ache. 'I should have noticed that something was wrong. She hasn't been herself for weeks now I come to think of it.'

'Don't blame yourself.' Sam's voice was deep and slightly roughened. It was the voice that turned millions of female viewers to jelly. 'I know you've had your work cut out covering for my father while he's been so ill. But now it's time to accept some help. You can't run the whole show by yourself, Riggs. No matter what you may think of yourself, you're not superwoman.'

She felt nothing like superwoman.

Anna's hand dropped into her lap. Suddenly she didn't have the energy to argue. 'All right.' Her voice was brisk and professional. 'We'll make the best of the situation. You take your father's surgeries but if you have any queries, you refer them to me.'

He arched an eyebrow. 'You think I can't cope?'

'I think it's been a long time since you've seen real patients. I'm not prepared for you to practise on mine.'

He would never admit he was wrong and she couldn't take that risk with people's lives.

'Fine. If I get stuck, I'll call.' His voice was a drawl and she had a feeling he was mocking her. 'Anything else?'

'We share the clinics and the house calls. The deputising service does the on call and weekends.' She took a deep breath. 'And any filming or fancy stuff that you want to do takes place outside surgery time.'

He gave a wry smile. 'Thanks for the welcome, Riggs.'

She stiffened. What did he want? Applause? 'If you're expecting a red carpet and a cheering crowd, you're not going to get one here.'

'Evidently.'

'And I'll sort out Glenda.'

'Her mother is my patient.'

'Your father's patient.'

He shrugged. 'Same thing. As you just said, I'm taking my father's patients.' He gave a humourless laugh as he realised what he'd just said. 'Following the old man's dream.'

'But not your dream, thank goodness.'

He lifted an eyebrow. 'Why "thank goodness"?'

'Because if you decided to take over your father's half of the practice permanently, we'd really be in trouble.' Frowning, Anna studied him. 'We can make this work because it's temporary, McKenna. Let's both remember that. Temporary.'

'If you think I'd want to make this a permanent arrangement then you're even more deranged than I already think you are.' He stifled a yawn and strolled out of the room as if he had all the time in the world, leaving her ready to punch something.

CHAPTER THREE

'SUBSIDENCE.'

'Sorry?' Anna juggled several bags and her mobile phone as she tried to concentrate on what the surveyor was saying. She still had one more house call to make before she finished for the evening.

'This cottage that you're hoping to buy has subsidence.' The man stepped back and angled his head. 'Didn't you notice that the windows are crooked?'

Anna followed his gaze, squinting against the bright evening sunshine. 'It's one of the reasons I fell in love with it. Crooked windows add to the character, Mike. They're what makes it quaint.'

'They're what makes it dangerous and a complete no-no for your mortgage company.' The surveyor looked at her sympathetically.

'I hope you're better at diagnosing patients than you are buildings, Doc. If this was an animal and you were a vet, you'd be putting it down.'

Anna groaned and dropped two of her bags. 'Mike, no! I don't need this. Tell me you're joking. You have to be joking. This is my new home.'

Her dream.

Her cottage by the beach.

'Not joking.' He shook his head solemnly, stepping back to look at the cottage with a gloomy expression on his face. 'It's a bad lot, Anna, love. Let it go.'

'Let it go? No way.' Anna stuck out her chin at an angle that made the surveyor sigh.

'Determination and backbone isn't going to fix this one, I'm afraid. The only way this is going to be yours is if you put up all the cash yourself.'

Anna almost growled with frustration. 'You know I can't do that.'

'Or find a rich man.'

Anna kicked a stone at the mere thought. 'I don't attract rich men. Rich men want useless trophy wives who'll agree with everything they say.'

Mike laughed. 'Not much chance of that with you. In which case, I think you're looking at another house, Anna.'

Anna shook her head in denial and disbelief. 'But it's all going through. I've chosen the curtains...'

Mike shrugged. 'Hang them in your next house,' he advised, 'but you have to give this one a miss. It's a bundle of trouble.'

Anna closed her eyes and breathed deeply. Did nothing in her life ever go right any more?

'It isn't exactly that simple, is it? I sold my flat two weeks ago, Mike, on the strength of moving into this place. I've been lodging with the McKennas while I've been waiting for the sale to go through.'

And much as she loved their place, it wasn't the same as having somewhere of her own.

'And they're away for the summer so they'll be glad to have you in their house for the duration.'

'It was just temporary.' She ran her fingers through her dark hair in a gesture of frustration. 'Just a couple of weeks to tide me over.'

Anna looked at the little cottage that had been part of her dreams.

Subsidence.

For a moment she let the wild, romantic side of her that she rarely acknowledged enjoy a wonderful dream about somehow finding the money and moving in, despite the subsidence. Then the practical side took over. As it always did.

'OK.' Her voice was weary and resigned. 'So I'll tell the solicitors that it's all off. And I'll start house-hunting again. In the meantime, I'll have to find a place to rent.'

Damn, damn and double damn. With David away and her workload already ridiculously heavy, she didn't have time for house-hunting. And anyway, she didn't want any old house. She wanted this one. She'd coveted it for years.

'In the summer?' Mike snapped his brief-case shut and gave her a rueful smile. 'Forget it, love. No chance. Why not just stay on at the McKennas'?'

Because she wanted her own home.

And because Sam was there.

Anna bit her lip.

'I'll find a place to rent.' She lifted her chin in a gesture of pure determination that had Mike sighing.

Anyone who had known Anna Riggs as a child recognised that look, and it wasn't to be messed with.

'OK, well, good luck. And call me when you find your next place. I don't want you ripped off.'

Anna gave him a wan smile. 'Thanks, Mike. I think.'

It wasn't his fault he'd had to give her bad news and she knew he had her best interests at heart.

That was another benefit of living in a small community, she mused as she watched Mike walk back up the path towards his car. People looked out for each other. Cared. There was no way that would happen in a city. Where was the goodwill among strangers?

Acknowledging that all the goodwill in the world was unlikely to find her a place to rent at the peak of the tourist season, Anna carried her bags back to her car, made her last call and drove up the coast road to the McKennas'.

Their spectacular house sat on a curve in the bay, just steps from the beach. It was the best property for miles around and it had been the McKennas' home for ever. Usually she loved coming here. Just walking up the path and breathing in the sea air was enough to put her in a good mood.

Not today.

Today, Sam's low, black sports car was parked outside, a blatant statement of mas-

culine self-indulgence that irritated her beyond belief. Why couldn't he just drive a normal family car?

Because Sam McKenna wasn't a normal
family man.

He was a stallion on the loose. A lone male
who had no intention of attaching himself to
anything or anybody. And he was undoubtedly *not* going to be pleased to discover that
he'd just got himself a housemate. It would
seriously cramp his style.

Anna almost smiled at the thought. If living here for a while was going to irritate Sam,
maybe it wouldn't be such a bad thing after
all.

Bracing herself for conflict, she let herself
in and paused. The house was silent so she
opened the French windows that led from the
spacious sitting-room and walked onto the
bleached wooden deck that overlooked the
beach below. Squinting at the foaming
waves, she could see several surfers and gave
a short laugh. Undoubtedly one of them

would be Sam. He obviously hadn't wasted any time in enjoying the benefits of Cornwall. For a wild moment she was tempted to join him and then she remembered the calls she had to make and the stack of medical journals that she was determined to at least scan before tomorrow.

Feeling uncomfortably sticky from her long working day and the warm weather, Anna showered quickly and washed her hair. Then she pulled on a pair of skimpy shorts, an equally skimpy top, poured herself a cold drink and walked onto the terrace to catch up on some reading.

'Nice to know you couldn't stay away from me, Riggs.'

She dropped the medical journal she was reading and registered the time with a twinge of shock. It was always like that with her. She became so absorbed in what she was reading that the world outside ceased to exist.

She glanced up at Sam, at the broad shoulders clearly outlined by the wet suit, at the growth of stubble on his hard jaw. He looked wickedly handsome and the long, leisurely look he gave her irritated her in the extreme.

No matter that they couldn't stand the sight of each other. If it was female, he still had to look. He just couldn't help himself.

'Stop staring, McKenna.' She gave him a frosty stare. 'I'm not one of your bimbos.'

He gave her a maddening grin, water dripping from his dark hair onto his wet suit. 'You've got good legs, Riggs. Always have had. But fortunately for both of us the rest of you is questionable so I'm able to resist you. I prefer my women gentle and cuddly.'

'You prefer your women brainless.'

He reached for a towel which he'd slung over the back of a chair in readiness for his return. ' "Soft" is the word I'd choose. Soft and yielding. You're more like a cactus. A man could get injured touching you.'

'If you touched me then you'd definitely be injured.' She angled her head and shot him a warning glance. 'And if being a cactus keeps you away, that's fine by me.' Feeling unaccountably warm under his lazy gaze, she glared at him. 'I suppose you're wondering why I'm here.'

He wandered back into the house and returned with a cold beer. 'I know why you're here.' He lifted the bottle to his lips and drank deeply, the muscles in his throat working as he swallowed. 'You find me irresistible. Don't worry about it. Women often do. You'll learn to live with the feeling.'

Anna glanced down at the beach below them. 'Just how far is the drop from here?'

He gave an appreciative grin and set the beer down on the table. 'Far enough. Why?' He lifted an eyebrow. 'Do you want to give it a go?'

She gritted her teeth. 'Don't tempt me, McKenna. If you have any concern for your safety, you'll drink that beer somewhere else.'

His grin widened. 'Trouble is, this is *my* home, Riggs, and you're the one sitting on my deck.'

'It's your parents' deck. And, believe me, I wouldn't be here unless there was a crisis.'

'My parents love having you. You're like a daughter to them.' He reached for the beer again. 'So what's the crisis?'

She bit her lip. She hated even saying the words. Hadn't got used to the idea herself yet. 'My house purchase has fallen through.'

He frowned. 'You sold your flat? What was wrong with it?'

'I wanted something bigger. Somewhere nearer the sea.'

'Yeah. You always did dream about that. Living virtually on the sand. Another one of your plans.' His eyes narrowed and he glanced at the view from his parents' deck. 'And maybe I don't blame you for that. I have to admit, it doesn't get much better than this.'

'It's a perfect spot,' Anna agreed, 'so why are you in London?'

He lifted the beer to his lips. 'Because there's more to life than a good view and a swim in the surf, Riggs. So where was the house? The one that you were hoping to buy?'

'Tub's Creek.'

'Old Jack Lawson's place?'

Anna nodded. Of course Sam would remember. He'd been brought up here, just like her. 'He died six months ago. Had a massive heart attack just after Christmas.'

'Not surprised with all the smoking, eating and drinking he usually did.' Sam gave a rueful smile. 'I think we can safely say that he lived life to the full. What was wrong with the cottage? Subsidence?'

Anna's jaw fell. 'How do you know?'

He shrugged. 'Common sense. It was pretty old and the windows were wonky. Had to be something.'

Anna sighed. 'I thought wonky windows gave a place character.'

'And major structural problems,' Sam said dryly. 'So now you're homeless.'

'I completed on the flat two weeks ago. It was that or lose the sale. I was expecting to exchange and complete in two weeks. It never occurred to me that there'd be a problem that I couldn't cope with. I was ready to buy it regardless.'

Sam shrugged broad shoulders. 'So buy it.'

'With what?' Anna shot him an impatient look. 'I need a mortgage and unfortunately people don't lend you money on wrecks.'

'Find somewhere new. Somewhere with straight windows.'

'Given the fact your father has landed me with a dud locum, I won't have the time to trawl estate agents. I'll rent for now.'

He ignored the dig and lifted an eyebrow. 'Rent? You're kidding. How do you expect to find somewhere to rent at this time of year? Every inch of available bed space is already let out to tourists. You wouldn't even find a stable.'

'All right, well, I'll sleep in the surgery if I have to,' she said irritably, and he yawned.

'Why would you need to? You can sleep here as far as I'm concerned. With six bedrooms, the house is big enough for both of us. You'll just have to try and resist me.'

'Believe me, no house would ever be big enough for both of us. Your ego takes up too much space.'

'Don't push your luck.' He finished the beer. 'I'm trying to be generous and giving here. If you're going to argue, you can sleep on the damned beach.'

'Sorry.' Something that she couldn't identify made her suddenly need to apologise. She ran a hand through her hair which had dried sleek and straight. It fell past her shoulders, halfway down her back. 'I'm just disappointed about the house. Worried about your dad. Anxious about the practice.'

Unsettled.

'Scared about the future.' Sam's gaze fixed on hers. 'Safe Anna. Careful Anna. Anna the planner. So ballsy on the outside but on the inside you crave security.'

She bit her lip, hating the fact that he knew her so well.

'Spare me the amateur psychology. Anyway, what's wrong with planning? And what's wrong with enjoying life and wanting it to stay the same?'

'Nothing. But think what you could be missing.'

She frowned. 'There's nothing missing in my life.'

'Apart from a social life.'

'I have a perfectly satisfactory social life, thank you.'

He leaned against the balcony, the wet suit lovingly displaying every muscular curve of his body. 'Bingo on a Friday, lobster night at the Dog and Duck. The beach barbecue. Take-away seafood from Hilda's Kitchen. Wow.'

'Never underestimate Hilda's seafood.' Anna clamped her jaw shut to prevent herself from rising to the bait. It was true that her social life was pathetically limited but that was as much because she was exhausted all the time as to lack of opportunity. By the time she finished work all she had the energy for was a date with a good book. But that was fine for now. She was busy establishing herself as a GP. Time for the rest later. It was all part of her life plan.

She leaned back in her chair and pretended to enjoy the view. 'At least my social life doesn't make the newspapers. Face it, McKenna, you just can't settle down with one woman, can you?'

Every time she saw a picture of him, he had a different woman on his arm. Usually blonde. Usually extremely curvaceous. None of them looked like the marrying type.

'Why would I want to?'

'Your mother is waiting for grandchildren.'

He threw his head back and laughed, a rich masculine sound that triggered an answering feminine response deep inside her. 'I hope she's a slow knitter.'

Suddenly Anna found herself noticing the tiny creases around his eyes and the way his jaw flexed when he smiled.

Disturbed by such unusually intimate observations, she rose to her feet and walked towards the house. His voice stopped her in the doorway.

'So, what are we eating tonight, Riggs?'

She turned back to face him, one brow arched in question. 'How would I know?'

'Perhaps because you've been living here for a few weeks? Presumably you've filled the fridge? Planned a few meals? Surprise me.'

She smiled sweetly. 'You've been reading fairy tales again. I'm not Little Red Riding Hood and you're every bit as capable of making a meal as I am. Probably more. You know where the fridge is, McKenna. If you want to eat, eat. Don't involve me in it.'

She hated to cook, even for herself. There was no way she'd be cooking for Sam. Unless she was aiming to poison him.

'Well, presumably you have to eat at some point, too.'

She leaned against the door-frame, her dark hair tumbling over her shoulders, her legs long and lightly tanned. 'I don't see why my eating habits are of any interest to you.'

'It's just that if you're cooking, it's as easy to cook for two as one.'

'If you're hoping I'm going to cook for you then you don't know me as well as I thought you did.'

Those blue eyes flashed a challenge. 'Eating is supposed to be an opportunity for social interaction between people.'

'People who like each other, McKenna. We don't. All the more reason for us to eat alone.'

He straightened up, his body lithe and powerful, stretching his shoulders to relieve the tension. 'All right. You never did quite have the woman thing sorted. So it looks as though I'm cooking.'

'Wait a minute.' Despite her vow not to rise to the bait, she couldn't stay silent. 'I've had enough of your digs for one night. What do you mean, I never did quite have the woman thing sorted?'

He hooked the empty beer bottle with his finger, his movements slow and casual. 'You just don't do woman stuff, do you? Never have.'

'Woman stuff? What woman stuff? You want me to dress in pink?'

He grinned. 'Can't see you in pink some-how.'

She made a mental note to buy something pink at the earliest opportunity. 'So what exactly do you mean?'

He shrugged. 'You don't cook. You don't play house. You just don't do girly stuff.'

Girly stuff?

Annoyed that he'd managed to make her feel inadequate, she glared at him. 'I have a full-time job, McKenna. And I eat perfectly healthy food—'

'Sandwiches.'

'I happen to like sandwiches. And I have a cleaner to do the house stuff. Or at least I did before I sold my flat. What you really mean is that you don't want a woman with an opinion.'

'*An* opinion?' He laughed. 'You've got so many opinions, honey, that talking to you is like negotiating an obstacle course.'

'Oh, for goodness' sake.' She frowned in irritation. 'It'll be a treat for you to hang around with someone who isn't a bimbo for a while. If you get really lucky I might talk to you from time to time about something other than facials and pedicures. And don't call me honey. It's completely demeaning and it winds me up.'

'That's why I do it.' He smiled smugly and strolled past her towards the kitchen. 'All right, this once I'll cook for you. But don't get used to it. If we're going to live together, you'll have to contribute. If you like, you can wash my socks.'

'Shame the camera isn't running,' Anna said tartly. 'I would have liked my response to that suggestion recorded for the nation's entertainment. And talking of cameras, if you're seriously going to stay and try and make this thing work, we need to talk.'

'More ground rules?'

'Just a few observations about the way things are going to be. I'll dump these journals in my room and I'll meet you in the kitchen. We can go through a few things.'

'Will you be wearing black leather and carrying a whip? I love it when you're dominating.' He unzipped the neck of his wet suit and Anna felt her breath catch and something slow and dangerous uncurl low in her pelvis.

Damn. Immediately she turned on her heel and strode out of the room, cursing her female hormones.

How could you react to a man that you didn't even like?

She of all people, who was so much more interested in the human mind than the human body.

She dumped the magazines on the bed with an impatient sigh. Unfortunately for her, Sam had an incredible body. And he knew it. But fortunately for her, she didn't like the man. So she was safe.

She sucked in a breath, gathered her thoughts back on track and mentally sketched out a few plans for how they could work together most efficiently. How they could work together with minimum contact.

When she marched into the kitchen fifteen minutes later she was armed with a notepad and determination not to let him unsettle her otherwise perfectly ordered life.

Despite the fact that she'd been quick, he'd already showered and changed and was dressed in a pair of cut-off jeans and a T-shirt which clung lovingly to the muscles of his broad shoulders. He was standing at the granite work surface, chopping vegetables with the speed and skill of a surgeon. For a moment she stood still, fascinated by those long, strong fingers and his sure touch.

Then she pulled herself together, dropped onto the nearest kitchen chair and blew a strand of hair out of her eyes. 'It's hot.'

'Yeah—stuffy. Good night for skinny-dipping.'

Anna sighed. 'Will you ever grow up?'

'If growing up means coming down here with a notepad and an official expression then I sincerely hope not.' He tossed slices of spring onion and ginger into a wok and waited while they sizzled. 'OK, Captain Riggs. Let's have it. Outline the plan of attack.'

Just being in the same room as him made her temper sizzle.

'You can mock all you like.' Her hair fell forward, brushing the table. 'But how do you think we're ever going to work together and deliver a reasonable standard of care for our patients if we don't do some planning?'

He added chicken to the wok. 'Do you plan with Dad?'

'We'd have meetings, yes.' She tapped her pen on the pad. 'But he and I have worked together for a long time. We know each other.'

Sam lowered the heat. 'We know each other, too, Riggs.'

'Too well.'

'Maybe.' He glanced towards her. 'Or maybe we'll both get some surprises. Life does that to you sometimes. Just when you think you've got it all worked out, the unexpected happens.'

He could say that again.

'You coming back to Cornwall is certainly unexpected,' she agreed, frowning as he handed her a glass. 'What's this?'

'An extremely good Sancerre. Excellent for hot weather and it will go well with my stir-fry. It might also soften your mood.'

'There's nothing wrong with my mood.'

He shot her a look. 'Just try it.'

She did and had to stop herself moaning out loud with sheer pleasure. It was cool and sharp and the alcohol oozed into her tired bones with immediate effect.

'It's good.'

'A lot of the things I do are good, Riggs. You ought to try a few more of them.'

She ignored the dig, set the glass down on the table and picked up the pen. 'I thought I could start by running you through some of the clinics that we do. You can tell me what you're comfortable with. I don't want you working outside your comfort zone.'

'You're questioning my abilities as a doctor again, Riggs.' He scraped the pan viciously to loosen the stir-fry. 'And it's only fair to tell you that it really ticks me off.'

She cursed men and their egos.

'You're being ridiculously sensitive,' she said stiffly. 'You haven't worked as a proper doctor for so long it's only natural that there are going to be areas that you're less experienced in. Obstetrics, for example. We have a ridiculous number of teenage pregnancies here. And emergencies. You know how far it

is to the local hospital and how many accidents we get on the beach every day in the
summer. Our surgeries are crammed with
them.'

'You should run an emergency surgery for
the tourists. It would save them traipsing
miles to the hospital or filling up surgery time
with minor accidents. I've suggested it to
Dad before.'

So had she, on numerous occasions, but
she wasn't going to let him know that.

'What we do now works perfectly well.'

He shrugged. 'Maybe. And maybe it
would work even better if you designated
some time to doing an emergency surgery.
You should have done it ages ago.'

He was completely right. 'We'll end up en-
couraging the tourists to come and see us
with every bump and bruise.'

'That's my father talking.' His gaze flickered to hers, challenging. 'You don't really
believe that.'

It was completely true. She didn't believe that. She thought it was a great idea. Always had. 'We'll see. It's only the start of the summer.'

'Fine. But it's the best plan.'

Anna frowned and tapped her pen on the pad. 'Let's look at practicalities. What this job is going to mean for you. It must be a while since you stitched a patient.'

'I think if I rack my brains it will all come back to me. I don't need tuition.' He lifted the wok and divided the contents between two plates. 'Here. Stop organising for one minute and eat.'

'Organisation is what keeps this show running.' But Anna pushed the pad to one side and reached for her wine. 'So when did you learn to cook?'

He handed her a plate piled high with food and a fork. 'I learned to cook when I decided that I liked eating decent food.'

'I'm surprised you don't just call on one of your women to cook whenever you're hungry.' She picked up her fork and stabbed some chicken and vegetables. 'Isn't that what primitive caveman is supposed to do?'

'This particular caveman can find plenty of other occupations for his women.' His eyes glittered slightly as he surveyed her over the rim of his glass. 'I don't want them wasting their energy in the kitchen.'

'You're a complete Neanderthal.' She felt the colour rise in her face and hated herself for being so sensitive to his comments. Particularly as she knew they were designed to wind her up. 'And I still think you should brush up on your emergency medicine.'

He topped up his glass. 'If we ran an emergency clinic it would make great television. The type of medical problems you're likely to encounter on your average beach holiday.'

'Oh, now I see why you're so keen to do it. Real-life casualties for your programme.' She twirled noodles around her fork. 'A bit of blood and gore will lift your image no end.

Dr Handsome doesn't just know about in-growing toenails—he can even save lives.'

He lounged back in his chair, his expression mocking. 'Never knew you thought me handsome, Riggs.'

She took a mouthful and shrugged carelessly. 'Well, fortunately for both of us, I'm not as shallow as the women you date. You look all right on the outside but it's what's on the inside that interests me and you just don't grab my attention, McKenna. Never have done. Never will do.'

He leaned forward, his gaze suddenly intent on her face. 'Is that a challenge?'

She looked at him, appalled. 'Of course it wasn't a challenge. Just the thought of you and I together is completely ludicrous.'

'That's right.' His fingers played with the glass. 'It is.'

'Exactly.' Something in his blue gaze was making her feel horribly uncomfortable. It was probably just the topic of conversation.

'All right, we'll do an emergency surgery from next week.'

'You're saying I'm right.'

'I'm saying we'll try it. Glenda can do a poster on the computer. We'll see how you get on.'

'Testing me?'

'Just looking out for my patients.'

He drained his glass. 'And when I prove to you that I'm perfectly competent, do I get an apology?'

'No, you get to see patients without me looking over your shoulder.'

'You certainly know how to deliver an incentive.' He put the empty glass down on the table. 'It's going to be a joy to work with you, Riggs.'

'Follow the rules, McKenna, and we just might survive.'

CHAPTER FOUR

THE first thing Sam saw when he walked into the surgery the next morning was a sensational pair of legs. Slim, brown and long enough to make a man forget what was in his head.

For a moment he just looked, and then he reminded himself of the price attached to admiring those particular legs.

Anna was leaning over the reception desk to grab a pen and the movement revealed enough of her to heat his blood.

'Good morning, Riggs. Nice skirt.'

He told himself that he could admire her legs without having to admire her as a person.

'You're late,' she snapped, straightening up so fast she almost lost her balance. It gave him some satisfaction to see that he'd flustered her.

'Not late.' He dragged his gaze away from those legs and glanced at the clock. 'On time. Punctual. And there's a queue at your door.'

'There's always a queue,' Anna said wearily, nodding at Glenda. 'OK, let's unlock the doors and get started.'

Sam took a good look at Glenda. Her hair wasn't combed and she hadn't bothered with lipstick. As long as he'd known her, Glenda had always worn lipstick. Something was definitely wrong. 'Polly, my producer, wants to come and look round and discuss some ideas over our lunch-break. Are you free, Riggs?'

Anna balanced a pile of papers under one arm and reached for her coffee with the other. Her black hair hung down her back, as glossy and shiny as silk. With her slanting brown eyes, she reminded him of a sleek cat. 'I don't have time for a lunch-break. And neither will you if you're intending to pull your weight.'

He ground his teeth and decided that even legs as good as those couldn't make up for the sharp tongue and the bossy nature. 'Not eating just shows poor time management.'

'I didn't say I didn't eat. Just that I don't take a lunch-break. That's a luxury we can't afford in the summer. If you want lunch-breaks, hang around until winter when the tourists leave.'

'I'm meeting Polly and we're starting filming this afternoon,' he said calmly, wondering whether the urge to strangle her had always been this powerful or whether it had just got a great deal worse. 'If you want to have some input, you might like to be there.'

She turned to face him, her head slightly tilted. 'This is why it is never going to work. Before you arrived I was struggling to cope with the workload and now, thanks to your perpetual need to have your ego stoked, I also have to cope with advising you on where to put your camera.'

He clamped his jaw to prevent himself saying that he knew exactly where he wanted to put the camera at this precise moment.

'OK, Riggs.' He ran a hand along the back of his neck and exercised his temper control skills. 'First of all, I know you've been struggling to cope but that's because Dad has been limping along at half-pace for months. Now I'm here and I'm more than capable of picking up all his work and probably some of yours.'

'I don't need you to touch mine—'

'I'm merely pointing out that I have the capacity to do so. The second point is that once we know what we're doing, the filming is surprisingly unobtrusive. We're filming normal, everyday surgeries. Despite what you think, nothing is staged for the cameras.'

'It'll probably take several takes to get your stitches straight.'

He wondered how many stitches it would take to sew her mouth up. He took a deep breath. 'You think I'm going to undo a wound and do it up again?'

She shrugged. 'How do I know to what lengths you'd go to make yourself look good?'

'That's why I'm inviting you to join this meeting.' He kept his voice even. 'Then you'll know. You might even enjoy it.'

She looked at him and then nodded. 'All right. I'll listen in. But only because I don't want things going on in my surgery that I don't know about. And I have to do the house calls first.'

'Fine. We'll arrange some sandwiches for after that.'

'I carry my mobile,' she said crisply, 'so if you need to consult on anything, you can call.'

'I'll remember that.'

Damn, the man was annoying!

The emergency surgery was a good idea. She'd suggested it herself, months ago, but

David had been resistant to changing their current set-up. In fact, he was pretty reluctant to institute any changes at all. He and her father had run the practice a certain way and since she'd joined him as his partner, David had expected her to fit in.

Anna frowned. To begin with that had been fine. She'd been finding her feet as a new GP and had been only too grateful to fall into a familiar structure. But as she gained confidence she'd seen things—things that needed to be changed. Things that would have improved the care for their patients.

But she'd learned to sneak changes in gradually, and the emergency surgery wasn't one that she'd tackled for a while. Unfortunately Sam was right about that one. She should have done it ages ago.

Then he wouldn't have had the satisfaction of thinking that it was his idea. She hated it when he was right about anything.

But one thing he wasn't right about was the filming, she told herself firmly. It would seriously disrupt the practice and make the patients feel uncomfortable.

She pondered the subject all the way through morning surgery, all the way through her house calls and all the way back to the surgery.

By the time she walked into the bright, airy reception area, she'd made up her mind that the whole thing was a mistake.

And leaving Sam alone had been a mistake, too. She should never have allowed him to finish his surgery without her there. What if something had happened? Something that he wasn't qualified to handle? He was too arrogant to admit that he needed help and he'd probably got himself into serious difficulties. David had one or two tricky patients.

Preoccupied with these thoughts, it came as a serious surprise to her to find Sam laughing with Glenda as the receptionist tidied up from the morning.

He didn't look like a man who'd had a stressful morning.

Anna dropped her bag and looked at him expectantly. 'So how was your surgery?'

'Good. There were one or two cases that would have made interesting television.'

She shot him an impatient look. 'Do you think of everything in terms of camera angles?'

'Not everything, no.' He winked at her suggestively. 'Just my work.'

She chose to ignore that, just as she chose to ignore most of the things he said. 'See anything interesting?'

'Fiona Walker's dog has been on the rampage again.' He rolled his eyes. 'One day she'll learn that it isn't the sweet little thing she thinks it is.'

Anna winced. 'That dog has kept her going since her Bill died last year.'

'I know that,' Sam said steadily, 'but it needs a muzzle. Fortunately the bite wasn't severe. They wanted to report it to the police but I promised that I'd talk to Mrs Walker.'

'You did?' Anna couldn't hide her surprise. 'Why would you do that?'

'Because, as you said, that dog is her life.'

'You don't know anything about her life.'

'I was brought up here, same as you and my mother writes to me,' Sam reminded her dryly. 'Endless gossip about harbour life. I know everything about everyone, not just Mrs Walker. I know that Doris in the gift shop had her gall-bladder out last winter, I know that her mother and grandmother have both had hip replacements and that the Stevensons are getting a divorce. I know that Hilda still gets eczema and Nicola Hunt is—'

'All right, all right.' Anna cut him off, hiding her surprise. 'I just didn't think those sort of details interested you.'

'All part of harbour life.'

'And you hate harbour life. That's why you choose to live in London.'

Sam gave an implacable smile. 'But I'm here now. And those are the details that you need as a family doctor. Those are the details that we're going to bring out in the programme. The way that we care for generations of the same family.'

'You mean that the way your father and I care for generations of the same family.'

Before he could answer the doors to the surgery crashed open and a man shouldered his way in, a child cradled in his arms, a frantic expression on his face. 'Quickly! I need a doctor. Someone help me—she's really struggling to breathe.'

'What happened, John?' Anna was beside him instantly, a brief examination of the child revealing that her lips were swollen and that she was wheezing badly.

'She's got a rash,' Sam murmured from next to her, his large hands lifting the child's T-shirt and exposing her abdomen. 'This is anaphylactic shock. I wonder what's caused it.'

'Let's get her into my consulting room.'

'I'll get the drugs.'

Acting as smoothly and efficiently as if they'd worked together all their lives, they swung into action.

'Do you know what happened, John? Any clues at all?' Anna questioned the father as she took the child and laid her on the examination couch, trying to obtain a history that might help them work out what had happened.

John was frantic, both hands locked in his hair as he watched helplessly. 'I don't know. God, I just don't know. We were on the beach, having a picnic—'

'What were you eating?' Anna took the oxygen mask from Sam and covered the child's mouth and nose while Sam adjusted the flow. 'Any food she hasn't eaten before? Nuts maybe? Strawberries?'

'No nuts. Hell— I don't know what she ate. All the usual stuff, I suppose.' He ran a hand over the back of his neck, his brow beaded with sweat. Then he glanced towards the door. 'Michelle will know. She's following with the baby. I came with Lucy because I can run faster.' He took several shallow breaths, fighting for control. Struggling to be strong in the face of a crisis. When he wasn't doing his job as a carpenter, John was the helmsman of the lifeboat and well used to dealing with emergencies. Just not in his own family. 'Crisps. She ate crisps. I remember that because Michelle was nagging her to eat a sandwich.'

Sam attached a pulse oximeter to Lucy's finger and checked the reading. 'Her oxygen saturation is 90 per cent.'

'Is that OK?' John glanced between them, anxious for information. 'Tell me that's OK. Tell me she's going to be OK.'

'We'd like it to be a little higher, but the oxygen will help,' Anna said calmly, holding the mask and stroking the little girl's head to try and calm her. 'Better give her some adrenaline and hydrocortisone, McKenna.'

'Ahead of you, Riggs.' Within seconds Sam had given the little girl an injection of adrenaline into her muscle. 'I'm going to put a line in. I have a feeling we might need it.'

Without question Anna handed him the necessary equipment and then examined the little girl's arm. 'This looks like a good vein.' She slipped on the tourniquet, tightened it and then shifted her position to allow Sam access.

In one swift movement he slipped the needle into the vein. No fumbling. No hesitation.

Anna hid her surprise. For someone who was out of practice, he hadn't seemed remotely hesitant. And he hadn't missed. She had to admit she was impressed. And relieved.

'Here…' She reached for some strapping to secure it. 'Don't want to lose that.'

'Right.' With a steady hand Sam gave the hydrocortisone and Anna checked the pulse oximeter again.

'Her sats are up to 94 per cent. Her breathing seems a little easier.'

'That's good. Let's see if this helps.' He gave the hydrocortisone and at that moment the door opened and Lucy's mother hurried in, white-faced and out of breath.

'Glenda's taken the baby for me. Is Lucy OK? What's wrong with her? She was fine one minute and then she just collapsed.' The questions tumbled out of her and, satisfied that Sam had Lucy under control, Anna hurried over to the distraught Michelle.

'She seems to have had an allergic reaction to something, but the drugs are helping. We need to know what caused it, Michelle. What were you doing when it happened?'

Michelle Craddock looked at her helplessly, her face shiny from the heat, her hair damp from running. 'Eating a picnic. Nothing exciting or dangerous. I just don't understand what could possibly have happened.'

'Could she have picked something up from the beach?' Sam dropped the empty syringe onto the trolley and glanced at Anna with a question in his eyes. 'Drugs?'

Her gaze held his. They both knew that during the summer months teenagers congregated on the beach in the evenings. The local police did their best to keep things under control but the odd broken bottle and syringe had been cleaned up the following morning by vigilant locals. Had the little girl picked something up from the sand?

Michelle was shaking her head. 'She didn't wander from the picnic rug. I would have noticed if she'd picked something up.'

'Her vital signs are improving and her sats are good,' Sam murmured, keeping a close eye on the child.

Anna was still questioning the mother. 'What was the very last thing she was doing before she collapsed, Michelle? Try and think. It could be very important.'

'Eating the picnic.' Michelle glanced at her husband for help. 'She was eating a ham sandwich, I think. No, it was crisps. Because I was nagging her about not touching the healthy stuff.'

John frowned. 'Actually, that's wrong, too.' His brow cleared. 'She was drinking, Miche. I remember now because her crisps fell onto the sand when she reached for her can.'

Sam glanced up. 'Can?'

'Fizzy drink.'

Sam's eyes narrowed. 'Had the can been open for a while?'

Michelle bit her lip. 'Not really. A few minutes, I suppose. She'd certainly had a few sips from it. Why?'

Anna picked up the questioning, following Sam's train of thought. 'And did she drink straight from the can?'

Michelle nodded, her expression anxious. 'Why? Why would that make her ill?'

'Because wasps crawl into cans of fizzy drink,' Sam said grimly, turning back to the child and checking her mouth and throat. 'Our guess is that she may have swallowed a wasp.'

'Oh, my God.' John's face was pale. 'You think she's been stung in her throat?'

'Possibly.'

John closed his eyes briefly and then looked at his wife and shook his head. 'We had no idea.'

'Lucky you brought her here as quickly as you did,' Sam said. 'Her breathing is improving and her heart rate is good. We'll get her transferred to the hospital and they'll keep her in overnight just to be sure.'

'Keep her in?' Michelle stroked Lucy's hair to keep her calm. 'But if she's better…?'

'There's a chance she might have a relapse,' Anna explained, glancing towards the window. 'I can hear the ambulance now. We'll transfer her to hospital and they can take a good look at her throat.'

'A wasp in the can. I can't believe I didn't think of that,' Michelle groaned, shaking her head in disbelief. 'And I think I'm such a careful mother.'

'Accidents still happen, Michelle, and you're a great mother,' Anna said quietly, walking towards the door as the paramedics hurried in, guided by Glenda. 'Hi, Todd. We need to get this little one to hospital quickly.'

She explained what had happened, gave him a summary of the care they'd given and then looked at Sam. 'One of us ought to go in the ambulance with her. You or me?'

'I'll go,' Sam said immediately. 'You might be needed here. I'll grab a lift back from someone.'

Now that the immediate danger to the child had passed, Anna swept her dark hair away from her face and gave a reluctant grin. 'Good work, McKenna. Maybe you're not as rusty as I thought.'

'If that's supposed to be a compliment then I'd say you need more practice.' He returned the smile and straightened. 'You didn't do badly yourself, Riggs. Good teamwork.'

Teamwork.

She frowned, slightly unsettled to realise that that was exactly what had happened. They'd worked as a team. A very effective team. And it wasn't at all what she would have expected. In the pressure of an emergency there had been no dissention between them—in fact, they'd hardly needed to speak. Each had worked smoothly alongside the other, instinctively anticipating each other's needs.

And then she noticed the camera. Her smile faded. 'You've been filming? You filmed what just happened?'

A girl with a clipboard murmured something in the producer's ear and Polly smiled. 'It will make fantastic television. But obviously only with the family's permission. And I agree that it was amazing teamwork.' The producer stepped forward, an awed expression on her face. 'The two of you were so slick. It was like watching a medical drama! Better, because it was real.'

Anna gritted her teeth and Sam drew in a breath, clearly anticipating a problem. 'Anna—'

'You shouldn't have filmed without the patient's permission.'

'We put a notice up saying that anyone not wishing to be filmed simply has to say so.'

Anna glanced at the wall, scanned the notice and scowled. 'Well, the Craddocks weren't exactly reading the notices on the wall when they came in here, were they? They wouldn't even have seen it!'

John Craddock rubbed the back of his neck and cast a glance towards his daughter, who was now sitting on his wife's lap. 'Can't honestly say I mind if they show it, Dr Riggs. Not if it saves someone else. What do you think, Michelle?'

His wife gave a wavering smile. She was still very pale from the experience. 'To be honest, I'm only too pleased for other people to learn the risks of not drinking straight from cans in the summer. It had never even occurred to me. And I worry about everything when it comes to the kids!'

Anna released a breath, unable to argue with that. It was an important health education message, that was true, and something that people often overlooked in the summer months when the weather was hot and wasps were abundant. 'Well, I suppose if you don't mind…'

John grinned. 'Just tell me when it's going to be shown, so that I can tell everyone who knows me.'

'We'll certainly do that.' The producer smiled, standing to one side as the paramedics prepared to take Lucy to the hospital. 'It'll be part of our series on summer health.'

Sam picked up his bag, helped himself to a few extra pieces of equipment that he thought he might need and gave Anna a nod. 'I won't be long. I'll just hand over and then catch a lift back.'

'Fine. I've got paperwork to do anyway. We'll delay that lunch. If there's going to be a camera stuck in my face every time I turn round, I definitely want to be part of the discussion.'

In fact, they didn't need to delay lunch for long.

Sam was back within the hour and the news on Lucy was good. 'She's stable now but they're keeping her in overnight. Now, let's get on with the meeting before the sandwiches curl. Glenda, are you joining us for this?'

'Oh, Dr McKenna…' Slightly breathless, Glenda glanced at them nervously, her hand shaking slightly as she smoothed her hair. 'I was thinking of popping home in my lunchbreak, if that's all right with you. But I could come if you'd rather…'

'Not at all,' Sam said easily, giving her a smile that made Glenda visibly relax. 'Have a nice lunch. See you later.'

Glenda vanished through the door so hastily that her bag tangled on the handle. With a murmured exclamation she tugged it free and hurried off without looking back, clearly in a hurry and very flustered.

Sam's smile faded. 'There goes a very stressed woman.'

Anna nodded, pacing over to the window and watching as Glenda virtually sprinted down the street towards the harbour. She knew that the receptionist would be home within five minutes. But why the hurry?

'You're right,' she said quietly. 'Something is very wrong and I feel very guilty that it took you to point it out.'

Sam strolled across the reception area and stood next to her. 'Just one of the advantages of having an injection of fresh blood in the practice.'

'Don't.' She glanced up at him, her expression troubled. For once she wasn't in the mood to argue with him. 'It worries me that I didn't notice.'

'Why should you have noticed? You're not superwoman.' He lifted a hand and brushed a strand of dark hair away from her face. The gesture was so unexpected that she jumped as though she'd received an electric shock.

'Just because we've managed to be civil to each other for the past half an hour, don't think you can take liberties, McKenna.' Thoroughly unsettled by the sudden wild increase in her pulse rate, she glared at him and he glared back.

'Just clearing your vision, Riggs. You need a haircut or you're going to trip on the stairs.'

She resisted the temptation to lift a hand to her hair. She always wore her hair long and he knew it.

'You know, it would make for riveting television if you let us film the two of you working together for the whole series.' The voice of Polly came from behind them and they both turned. 'There's a tremendous chemistry between you. The room just pulses with energy whenever you're together. And the best thing is that you two don't even seem aware of it.'

Chemistry?

Anna gaped at her. 'The sort of chemistry that causes an explosion,' she muttered darkly, and Sam grinned.

'I don't think our Anna sees herself as a film star, Polly.'

The producer looked thoughtful. 'Well, a lot of people are resistant to the thought of being filmed but once they get used to it they usually find they forget about the cameras and just get on with the job. That's one of the reasons that these fly-on-the-wall documentaries are so successful. The viewers feel as though they're genuinely part of what's going on.' The producer tipped her head on one side and narrowed her eyes. 'Even without looking at what we just filmed, I can tell that you're going to look fabulous on camera. Gorgeous.'

Anna glared at both of them. 'I do not want to be filmed.'

'Fine by me.' Sam suppressed a yawn. 'Personally I think it would be pretty hard to find your good side anyway.'

The smooth working relationship was gone. Back was the constant needling.

'You are unbelievably shallow.'

Polly glanced between them and grinned. 'If you're both willing to suspend hostilities, the sandwiches are looking particularly tempting.'

'Yeah, we're ready.' Sam strolled across the reception area and made for the stairs that led to the staffroom.

Aware that the producer was still staring at them in fascination, Anna followed more self-consciously.

Chemistry.

It was utterly ridiculous to suggest that she and Sam shared any sort of chemistry. And as for looking good on the camera—the whole idea was totally ridiculous.

'It would be great if we could incorporate more of your accident and emergency skills, Sam,' Polly was saying as Anna grabbed a cup of coffee and took her seat at the table.

'I know we need the routine stuff, too, but a bit of that does get the adrenaline pumping.'

'What accident and emergency skills?' Anna helped herself to a sandwich. 'Since when did you have accident and emergency skills?' Then she remembered the calm, competent way he'd reacted to the crisis downstairs and something clicked in her brain. 'What jobs have you been doing in London, McKenna?'

Polly smiled. 'When he's not doing his usual surgery and working for us, he does nights at the A and E department of...' She named a busy London hospital and Anna put the sandwich back on her plate untouched, her eyes on Sam.

'You're working nights in an A and E department? Why?'

His eyes gleamed. 'So that my medical skills don't become as rusty as a garden fork, Riggs, that's why. We see a range of conditions in the London practice but there's nothing like nights in A and E to hone your skills.'

She stared at him. 'That explains why you were able to get that line into the child.'

'I've done it a few times, yes.'

She glared at him. 'You should have told me.'

'You shouldn't have assumed that I was useless.'

'Now, now, children.' Polly's expression was amused. 'It's always fun to watch the two of you in action, but we're already pushed for time so can we move on to the matter in hand? We need to discuss our plans for filming this summer.'

Anna bit hard into her sandwich and glared at Sam. But her anger with him for deliberately deceiving her was tinged with respect. The guy clearly knew what he was doing. And he was an impressive doctor.

It was just a shame that she wanted to strangle him.

*   *   *

That evening, despite the heat, Anna decided to go for a run on the beach. She always found exercise good for tension, and the tension in her life had rocketed ever since Sam had walked into her surgery.

Despite all their reassurances during the lunch-time meeting that the patients would love the idea of being 'on the telly', she still had serious reservations about filming. They'd agreed to seek permission from every patient but still Anna couldn't quite imagine that people would want their lives exposed on television. For herself, she couldn't think of anything worse. She liked her privacy too much and she never had been able to understand why some people craved public attention.

Despite the fact that it was past seven o'clock, the beach was still crowded with families and Anna jogged slowly down to the water's edge and then lengthened her stride, enjoying the cool breeze blowing off the sea.

This was a popular surfing beach and the water was still crowded with teenagers determined to make the most of the waves.

By the time she returned to the McKennas' house she was panting and uncomfortably hot. She ripped off her running gear and stepped straight under a cold shower, moaning with relief as the water cooled her heated flesh. Bliss. She was tempted to stay under the water all evening but her stomach was rumbling and she knew she had to eat something after such a long run.

She slipped on a short linen dress, padded down to the kitchen and opened the fridge.

'I cooked last night so I guess tonight has to be your turn.' Sam lounged in the doorway, a beer in his hand, watching her.

Anna turned. 'Has anyone ever told you that you look more like a beach bum than a doctor?'

His hair was slightly too long, his jaw rough with stubble and he wore a pair of long surf shorts and a loose T-shirt that clung to the powerful muscles of his shoulders.

He gave her a lopsided grin that made her heart kick uncomfortably against her chest. 'You want me to wear a suit and tie?'

'I don't care what you wear.' She yawned and turned back to the fridge. 'It isn't looking promising. The only thing I can cook is omelette and we're right out of eggs.'

Sam strolled over to her and peered over her shoulder. 'So you'd better buy me dinner.'

She wrinkled her nose and slammed the fridge shut, forcing him to step backwards or risk injury. 'Why should I buy you dinner?'

'Women fight to buy me dinner, Riggs.' He hooked his thumbs in the waistband of his shorts, his blue eyes mocking. 'This could be your lucky night. I'm making you an offer you shouldn't be able to refuse.'

Her heart kicked against her ribs and she wished he'd move away slightly. He was standing far too close.

'I have no trouble refusing.' But then her stomach rumbled and she remembered how hungry she was. And how empty the fridge was. 'On the other hand, I'm starving. What exactly did you have in mind?'

'That new place on the beach? Plates of seafood. Lashings of garlic butter. Chilled white wine.'

Anna felt her taste buds react with enthusiasm. 'I've heard good things about that place.' She tilted her head to one side and considered. 'And the only price is being civil to you for the duration?'

'Who said anything about being civil?' He lifted the bottle to his lips and drained the beer. 'Just be yourself.'

She glared at him. 'I'm civil with most people, McKenna. It's just you that drives me nuts.'

'And why is that, I wonder?' He put the bottle on the table and surveyed her, his eyes gleaming with speculation. 'Perhaps you're harbouring secret fantasies.'

'The heat must have gone to your brain.'

He lounged against the table, broad-shouldered and unreasonably handsome. 'Face it, Riggs. You have trouble resisting me. And that really annoys you.'

'You're the one who annoys me. And it's worse when I'm hungry. So let's get going before I commit bodily harm. You won't look so handsome with a black eye and no teeth.'

He reached for his car keys. 'In the interests of personal safety, I'll drive.'

She followed him to the curving gravel driveway and paused, a frown on her face as she looked at his sleek black car. 'You expect me to sit beside you in that sex machine?'

'Well, it's that or the boot, honey, because there's no room in the back. This is definitely a two-seater.'

She sighed and slid into the car, too hungry to argue. 'OK, but only because my stomach is more important to me than my reputation at this particular moment in time.'

She was starving.

He turned the key, started the engine and smiled. 'Don't you just love that sound?'

'It's an engine.'

He shot her a pitying look. 'No appreciation for the finer things in life, that's your problem.' He hit the accelerator, sending gravel flying. 'And what does sitting in my car have to do with your reputation?'

'If I'm seen with you then people will automatically think I'm a bimbo.' She scooped her hair out of her eyes and held it firmly at the back of her neck as he picked up speed and headed for the coast road. 'But to sample the lobster at that new restaurant, I'm willing to take the risk. And don't call me honey. I draw the line at that, even when I'm starving.'

The restaurant was heaving but the manager took one look at Sam and found them a secluded table overlooking the sea.

'Never miss one of your programmes. Love the way you make complicated medical stuff easy to understand. Pleasure to have you back, Sam.' The manager handed him a menu. 'And dining with our Dr Riggs. That's cosy.'

'Convenient, not cosy.' Anna shot him a pointed look and took the other menu. She didn't want gossip in the village. 'This is just business. We have things to talk about, we both have to eat and we both wanted to try your new place, Ken. It's that simple.'

'Well, the first drink is on the house. I'll treat you to a couple of glasses of champagne.' He snapped his fingers, gestured to a waiter and then turned back to the two of them. 'Been meaning to come and talk to your dad, actually, Sam. Something on my mind, to be honest.'

'Stop by any time,' Sam said easily, leaning back in his chair and closing the menu. 'I'm covering all Dad's surgeries now. Be glad to catch up with you.'

Ken nodded. 'I think I'll do that. Thanks.' At that moment one of the waiters arrived with two brimming glasses of champagne and Ken stepped to one side, giving Anna a quick wink. 'Have a nice evening, both of you.'

Anna watched him go and then lifted her champagne. 'Why was he winking at me? Has he developed a problem with his eye? And why all this man-to-man stuff about seeing you in the surgery? He could have come to see me.'

'There are some things a man can't discuss with a woman.'

'That's rubbish.' She swallowed a mouthful of champagne and moaned with appreciation. 'Ooh, that's fantastic. And, McKenna, I can deal with everything you can deal with. Probably more.'

'You know as well as I do that there are some things a woman prefers a woman doctor for. It's the same for men.'

Anna took another sip and felt her head swim. She put the glass down on the table and decided to wait for the food before drinking any more. Otherwise she'd be tipsy and she needed her wits about her to cope with Sam. 'That's why I always end up with the women's problems. Because you guys avoid them like the plague.'

'That's nonsense.' His tone was calm and he broke off to deliver their order to the waiter. Anna stared at him as the waiter left to give their order to the kitchen.

'I'm perfectly capable of reading a menu and using my voice. And for your information, I don't have any trouble with decision-making. I can pick my own food. If I concentrate I can even use a knife and fork.'

'We both want to try the seafood.' He spoke with exaggerated patience. 'I ordered seafood. Relax, will you?'

Despite her resolve, Anna reached for the champagne again. She couldn't relax around Sam. It just wasn't possible. 'You were trying to pretend that you don't avoid women's problems.'

'I certainly don't. In fact, it's an area that we cover frequently on the programme, as you'd know if you ever bothered to watch it.'

'I get enough of you in real life.'

He leaned forward, his blue eyes fixed on her face. 'It's a fact that lots of women prefer to see a female doctor for some things, and it's the same with male patients. If Ken wants to see me, you shouldn't be defensive about that.'

'I'm not being defensive.'

Damn. She wished she hadn't drunk all that champagne so quickly. She definitely should have waited for the food.

Fortunately it arrived quickly, huge plate-fuls of seafood with hot garlic butter and baskets of freshly baked bread.

'Oh, this looks fantastic,' Anna muttered, reaching for a langoustine and stripping it quickly. 'Great idea, McKenna. Beats omelette.'

'There were no eggs,' he reminded her. 'Omelette was never an option.'

'That's right.' She grabbed a napkin before the buttery juices could slide down her chin. 'No eggs. So someone needs to go shopping. I'll grab a few things tomorrow on my way home.'

He scooped another langoustine onto her plate. 'Are you offering to shop, Riggs? Something wrong?'

'I don't mind the shopping. It's the cooking I can't stand. And tonight I'm feeling mellow. Blame the alcohol and the food.'

'You really know how to make a guy feel good.'

'You don't need me to make you feel good. You already feel far too good about yourself. It would be much easier for the rest of us mortals if you'd let a little bit of self-doubt creep in. You need to lose some of those female fans and realise that you're human, like the rest of us.'

He looked at her thoughtfully. 'Do you suffer from self-doubt?'

She paused with a langoustine halfway to her mouth and then dropped it back on her plate. 'Yes. Of course I do. You try joining an established practice run by our respective parents. No matter how many times I prove myself, I'm still the child. I'm not capable of having an idea worth listening to.'

And it rankled. She knew she was a good doctor. She had ideas of her own. Ideas that she wanted to develop for the good of her patients. For the good of the whole practice.

Wondering why on earth she was telling him this when it wasn't something she ever voiced to anyone, she scowled and reached for her glass. Then she changed her mind and lifted her water instead. It was probably the alcohol that was making her so garrulous.

'Yes, I can imagine it must be hard. Dad hasn't let you make any changes, has he?' Sam wiped his fingers on a napkin. 'He can be a stubborn old guy when he wants to be. I'm amazed you haven't walked out before now. Spread your wings.'

'I feel a responsibility to give something back to this place. And I love your dad and I love the practice,' Anna said softly, turning her head and staring out across the sea. The sun had dipped behind the cliffs and streaks of scarlet shot across the sky, casting lights on the waves. On their table a candle flickered and a vase of sweet peas scented the air. For some reason Anna felt a lump building in her throat. 'And this is my home. I'd never want to work anywhere else. I don't know how you can bear London. Don't you miss it here?'

'Yes, of course I miss it.' His tone was equally soft and his eyes were locked on hers. 'It's my home every bit as much as it's your home. Yes, I miss it. But this place didn't give me what I needed.'

'And what was that?'

He stared into the candle, watching the breeze toy with the flame. 'Space to make my own discoveries. Freedom to make my own mistakes.' He shrugged and reached for his glass. 'I didn't want to just move into something that my father had built. That was his dream and I suppose I needed to follow my own dream. I needed something different.'

'Bright lights and adulation.'

He looked at her thoughtfully over the rim of his glass. 'You really don't think what I do rates very highly, do you?'

'You truly want to know what I think?'

'Just this once, yes, I'll risk it.' He put the glass down and sat back in his chair, eyes narrowed. 'Tell me what you think, Riggs.'

She took a deep breath. 'I think you're an extremely talented doctor who's wasting those talents. You could be making a real difference to people's lives. Saving lives. You did it this morning. Don't you miss that, Sam? That feeling of having really helped someone?'

His gaze didn't shift from hers. 'You don't think I help people?'

She shrugged, wishing that he'd look at his plate or his food. There was something about those killer blue eyes that she found more than a little disconcerting. 'I can see the job is glamorous.'

He leaned forward. 'In the last six months we've had dozens of letters from people whose lives have been changed by things they've seen on the programme. My programme. Sometimes it's life-saving stuff, Riggs. First-aid tips that come in useful. People remember them if they've seen them on television. And they use them. Sometimes it's something far less dramatic but no less important. We tackle subjects that some people find too embarrassing to discuss with their own doctors. And sometimes that gives them the courage to see their own doctors and sort out a problem that's limiting their lives. We make a difference.'

Anna stared at him. 'You're pretty passionate about it.'

'Very. I think it's a very useful method of patient education. These days patients want to be informed. They need to be informed.'

'That's all very well...' Anna picked at a piece of bread '...but from where I'm sitting there's nothing more irritating than a patient coming into the surgery clutching a magazine announcing the arrival of another wonder drug.'

'I'm not saying that all media reporting of health stories is good,' Sam said. 'I'm just saying that you shouldn't dismiss it. Watch my programme. Tell me that what we're doing in the surgery wouldn't make good summer viewing. There's a lot people could learn from us.'

'Well, I agree that the wasp message is a useful one,' Anna conceded, and Sam nodded.

'And what we need to do now is a piece talking about first aid for anaphylactic shock, how to recognise and deal with it. Remind people with known allergies to carry adrenaline.'

'I still think that the cameras will put patients off coming.'

'It won't put them off,' Sam predicted. 'It will attract them like magnets. Trust me on that one. You'd be amazed at the number of people who are only too delighted to air their health problems on national TV.'

He sat across from her, talking easily, making her laugh with outrageous stories, and when she finally looked at her watch she was astonished to find it was past midnight.

'Look at the time! I've got a pile of reading to do before I go to bed.'

He yawned and finished his coffee. 'Forget the reading for once. Have a night off.'

'I like to stay up to date and stuck down here in Cornwall in a two-man practice, I never get to conferences.'

He looked at her. 'Reading. Conferences. What about parties? Nights on the town? Don't you ever have doubts about devoting your life to medicine?'

She frowned and tilted her head to one side, her silken dark hair sliding over her shoulder and brushing the table. 'I'm not devoting my life. I'm twenty eight, not a hundred. This is just my focus for now. Not for ever.'

'Precisely. You're twenty-eight. You should have a sex life.'

She straightened her shoulders. 'My sex life is none of your business, McKenna, but just in case you haven't scrutinised the electoral role lately, I ought to warn you that there's a shortage of single, eligible men in this village. And I don't sleep with my patients.'

'Then spread your net wider.'

Her frown deepened. 'I'm quite happy as I am, for now. My plan is to carry on until I feel I've really grasped the job. Then maybe it'll be time for more personal stuff.'

'Anna the planner.' He lifted his glass and drained it, his eyes glittering slightly in the flickering candlelight. 'And what if fate intervenes? What if Mr Right arrives before you've scheduled him in to your life plan?'

She grinned airily. 'I'll probably be too busy reading my journals to notice him.' She waved a hand at Ken who was hovering at a nearby table, chatting to the diners. 'We're off, Ken. You'd better charge us for this feast while we're still sober enough to pay.'

Sam reached into his wallet for his credit card and Anna frowned. 'What's that for?'

'Well, unless you intend to spend the rest of the night in the kitchens, washing up, I was planning to pay.'

'You're not paying for me. We'll go halves.'

Sam yawned. 'For goodness' sake, Riggs. Can't you even let a guy buy you dinner?'

'I can buy my own dinner and this wasn't a date, McKenna. It was an alternative to omelette.'

Sam surveyed the pitiful remains of food on the table. 'It was a good alternative. Especially given that there were no eggs. And I'm paying.'

'That's just ridiculous.'

'No, that's just the way it is.' He handed his card to Ken. 'Fantastic food, Ken. Great evening. Make that appointment to see me any time.'

'Has anyone ever told you that you're stubborn and opinionated?' Anna rose to her feet and reached for her bag. 'Just for the record, your macho, he-man act doesn't work on me, McKenna. If you're expecting it to make my legs go weak, it's only fair to warn you that I'm still walking with no problems.'

'Really?' He pulled a face. 'Damn. I must be losing my touch. Need to lift a few more weights. Practise my walk. And for the record, you're more stubborn than me.'

They left the restaurant and walked back to the car.

'Now, this is when I love Cornwall.' Sam stopped and stared out across the darkened beach. The sea hissed as the waves hit the sand and behind them they could hear laughter from the restaurant. 'I love it when the tourists leave and the beach is ours again.'

Anna stood next to him. 'The trouble is nowadays the tourists never leave. Most of these beaches are as crowded at night as they are during the day. Once it gets dark the partying starts.'

They stared at a group of teenagers gathered at the water's edge and Sam frowned. 'The problem with this place is that the teenagers don't have anywhere to go. And there's no privacy. If one of them makes an appointment at the surgery, everyone knows.'

'What's wrong with that?'

'Well, if you're trying to be cool, or if you're trying to hide something from your parents, then making an appointment with us is like taking out an ad in the paper.'

Anna stared at him. 'You think that's why teenagers don't come?'

'One reason.' He looked at the group on the beach. 'We ought to start a teenage health group. Somewhere they can go, mingle and chat to a doctor if they want to.'

It was a great idea. 'No one would turn up.'

'They'd turn up if we made it cool.'

'And how would we do that?'

He turned and gave her a lopsided smile. 'I'd be the doctor.'

She grunted with exasperation. 'You are so arrogant.'

'What's the teenage pregnancy rate here?'

'It's high, as you well know.'

'Probably because if they go to the doctor, they broadcast the fact from the rooftops. If there was a clinic for teenagers, we could deal with all sorts of things. Drugs, eating disorders, contraception and the positive stuff, exercise, healthy eating.'

It was a fantastic idea. 'It would never work.'

'Let's try it. Send invitations to all the teenagers in the area.'

'I'll think about it.' She was definitely going to do it.

'You're afraid I'll be proved right.'

'You're never right, McKenna. And all our teenagers want to do is party.'

'Talking of parties, when is the beach barbecue to raise money for the lifeboat? Must be soon.'

Anna laughed. 'The highlight of our social calendar. I'm amazed you remember it.'

'It was at the beach barbecue that I finally scored with Daisy Forest,' Sam said smugly. 'Not likely to forget that in a hurry. What a girl.'

'Well, it's probably only fair to warn you that Daisy Forest is now a happily married woman with three little girls and a doting husband whose shoulder measurements exceed even yours. You might want to rethink that attachment.'

Sam winced and gave a wry smile. 'Damn. There go my dreams.'

'Just for my own interest and research, what was it that wrecked them? The three little girls or the dimensions of her husband?'

'Both. I'm a man who hates competition. So when is it?'

'The beach barbecue? Three weeks on Saturday. Usual fund-raising stuff. Ken does the food, there's dancing, several people get drunk and make fools of themselves. We raise some money, we buy new equipment. You know the sort of thing.'

'Sounds too good to miss.' He stood next to her, broad-shouldered and handsome. Sexy.

Anna scooped her hair away from her face and frowned. Since when had she ever found Sam McKenna sexy?

Obviously since she'd drunk too much champagne on an empty stomach. She was hallucinating. Her judgement was failing. It was time to go home.

'Do you want to leave the car and walk?'

He turned. 'Unlike you, I didn't indulge. I'm fine to drive. And I'll need the car in the morning.'

She yawned as they walked to the car park. 'So tomorrow filming starts in earnest?'

'Polly has all sorts of plans, but often we just see what comes in. What looks interesting.'

He drove back slowly and Anna closed her eyes, loving the feel of the wind in her hair. 'All right, you win. This is bliss. Not the engine, just the lack of roof.'

'Glad I've finally pleased you. Remind me to give you champagne more often,' Sam said dryly. 'You become more human.'

'With most people I'm human,' she murmured. 'It's just you that brings out the worst in me. Always have done, McKenna. Always will do.'

'We've done all right tonight.' He pulled up outside the house and they walked inside. 'No bloodshed. No visible wounds.'

They made their way to the kitchen and both of them reached for the light switch. Their fingers touched and suddenly she realised how close they were. She could feel the warmth of his breath near her face, feel the brush of his powerful body against hers. The lights flickered on and his gaze slid slowly to hers. Suddenly they were eye to eye and awareness shot between them like a bolt of lightning.

The breath caught in her throat and her heart bumped against her chest. 'Do you… want coffee?' Her voice sounded strange. Totally unlike her own. And she found herself noticing things about his eyes that she'd never noticed before. Like the fact that in this light they looked an even deeper blue. And that his lashes were thick and sinfully dark. Lashes that should have looked feminine but somehow made him more male than ever.

'Coffee?' His gaze slid to her mouth as if he was trying to make sense of something extremely complicated. 'I thought you were keen to get back to those journals of yours.'

'That's right.' She fought the temptation to lift her fingers to her lips, but his gaze fixed on her mouth was making her tingle. 'Journals.'

'No coffee, then.' His eyes lifted to hers and locked. 'I'll see you in the morning.'

'Presumably.'

Their fingers were still tangled together, still on the light switch, and they both pulled away at the same time, their bodies bumping together as they turned for the door.

'Hell, Riggs…' He hauled her against him and brought his mouth down on hers hard, one hand sliding behind her neck and holding her fast.

She fell into his kiss, drowning in the heat and the fire, a dangerous thrill curling upwards from deep inside her. It was hot and frantic and totally out of character, but for a brief moment in time she didn't care. She didn't care about the future and she didn't care about the past. She just wanted now.

She grabbed the front of his shirt to press herself closer, and without lifting his head he backed her against the wall, his kiss impossibly intimate, his hands sliding with sensual purpose up the sides of her body until they rested on her breasts. She felt the cool wall against her back, felt the press of solid muscle and hard, sexy male and closed her eyes.

When he finally dragged his mouth from hers and slid hot kisses down her throat, she gasped for air and struggled to rescue the situation.

'We should stop this.' Her eyes stayed closed and a soft gasp escaped from her lips as he jerked the strap of her dress down and trailed kisses over the swell of her breast. 'McKenna...' She groaned his name. 'I said we should stop.'

'We probably should.'

Her head tilted back as his lips moved lower still. 'This isn't a good idea.'

'Feels pretty good from where I am,' he murmured hoarsely, straightening and returning his full attention to her swollen mouth. 'Never thought you'd taste this good, Riggs. Incredible.'

She dragged her eyes open and tried to summon up some of the old feelings of irritation and exasperation. But all she could feel was heat.

She was in big trouble.

'We really can't do this. We have to stop.'

'Good idea.' His tongue slid into her mouth and he kissed her again. Then he lifted his mouth just enough to speak. 'We'll stop. Any minute now, we're going to stop this. God, you smell good.' He rubbed his face over her cheek. 'Have you always smelt this good or have I just not breathed you in before?'

She was aware of every single masculine inch of him, pumped up and virile and so devastatingly sexy that it was almost impossible for her to breathe. The wanting was so powerful that she couldn't think straight.

'You're going to have to stop this, McKenna.'

His mouth played with hers. Teasing. Tantalising. 'Not sure I can. You taste as good as you smell.'

'Then we'll both do it. On three. You move away. I move away.' She felt his tongue coaxing hers and she groaned and curled her fingers into the hard muscle of his forearms. 'I said, on three. One, two, three.'

She gave him a shove and he stepped backwards. It gave her some satisfaction to see that his breathing was decidedly unsteady. Hers was, too. If she had a patient in this state she'd be considering medication.

'OK, well, that worked.' She lifted the strap of her dress with shaking fingers and raked her tangled hair out of her eyes. She dreaded to think what she looked like but, judging from the look burning in his eyes, she decided it was probably better not to know. 'I'll just go to bed...'

He inhaled deeply. 'Just so that there's no misunderstanding here—on your own, I presume?'

'Definitely on my own.' She backed towards the door, her legs decidedly unsteady. 'And we're going to forget this happened.'

He raked long fingers through his already roughened hair. 'That easy, huh?'

'I didn't say it was going to be easy,' she said honestly, 'just that that is what we're going to do.'

'Unless we go with Plan B.'

'Which is?'

His eyes were on her mouth. 'We take this to its natural conclusion.'

The air stilled and her heart skipped a beat. 'I can't believe we're having this conversation. We drive each other crazy, McKenna.'

His eyes darkened. 'I think we've just proved that.'

'You know what I mean. We don't even like each other and I need to like a man before I take him to bed. It's the barest minimum requirement. And we can't even converse without annoying each other.'

'Riggs...' His voice was sexier than a man's voice had a right to be. 'At the moment, I'm not thinking about conversation.

I'm just thinking about your body in my bed. And more of what we just sampled.'

His words made her stomach flip. Her body in his bed. *His body tangled with her body.*

His shirt was half undone where she'd dragged at the bottom and she saw the haze of dark hair on his chest. He was a man designed to tempt a woman from the straight and narrow.

And she was tempted. So tempted.

'We'd regret it in the morning.'

'I never regret anything I do. It's a waste of emotion.'

'Look…' She scooped her hair away from her face and licked her lips, struggling to be rational. 'Let's just admit this was a mistake. We had a nice evening and that's rare for us. We both drank a bit too much.'

'I'm stone-cold sober.'

'We're going to forget it happened.' She ignored his soft statement and backed through the door, holding onto the wall for support. Ever since he'd kissed her, her legs didn't seem to be working that well.

'Riggs.' His voice stopped her before she made it to the stairs. 'What if we can't forget it happened?'

She paused, her hand curled tightly round the banister for safety. 'We will.'

They had to.

Otherwise they were in big trouble.

CHAPTER FIVE

THE following morning the surgery was crowded with patients and Anna was relieved that there was no sign of Sam. She couldn't face him at the moment. Not until she'd managed to wipe out all memories of that incredible kiss.

Chemistry.

Damn. Who would have thought it? It just went to prove that the mind and the body were totally incomprehensible.

'Glenda rang.' Hannah, the other receptionist, looked at Anna searchingly, clearly wondering what was wrong with her usually sharp-minded boss. 'She's been caught up at home but she'll be in as soon as possible.'

Anna frowned. Caught up with what? 'Fine. Do you know what's wrong, Hannah? Did she say anything?'

Hannah shook her head. 'No.' The young girl looked thoughtful. 'But she didn't sound herself. And she hung up in a hurry.'

'OK. Any sign of Dr McKenna?'

'He phoned just before you arrived to say that he was making one call on his way in and to explain to his patients.'

'Oh.' For a moment Anna was annoyed that he hadn't thought to call her on her mobile and tell her his plans. Then she remembered that she'd gone out of her way to avoid him that morning. She'd showered early, skipped breakfast and sneaked out of the house before she'd heard sounds from his bedroom. Presumably he'd taken the same approach and that was why he hadn't called her.

Which proved that her plan was the right one. Ignore the whole thing. Pretend it had never happened. They should never have indulged in that kiss and the sooner they both put it behind them and started to act normally again, the better for both of them.

'OK, Hannah, I'll get on with my surgery. Let me know when Dr McKenna arrives. If he's horribly delayed I'll tuck his patients in between mine.'

Her first patient was Katy, a seventeen-year-old who walked in with her mother. Anna took one look at the teenager's face and knew this was going to be a difficult consultation.

Sam was right. They needed a clinic for teenagers.

'Hello, Katy.' She offered the girl the seat closest to her and gave her mother a brief smile. 'Hello, Mrs Walker.'

'She doesn't want to be here,' Mrs Walker said briskly, 'but I've told her that if she doesn't come, I'll cut off her allowance.'

Anna winced mentally and glanced at Katy, gauging her reaction. The girl looked sullen and uncooperative but that was hardly surprising given the circumstances.

'She doesn't eat and she spends her life in the gym,' Mrs Walker began, her mouth tightening in disapproval as she looked at her daughter.

'At least I don't sit on the couch playing computer games,' Katy muttered, scowling at her mother. 'And there's nothing wrong with going to the gym. It's healthy.'

Anna thought for a moment and then smiled at Mrs Walker. 'Would you mind if I spoke to Katy alone?' She rose and walked to the door, leaving the mother no choice but to stand up and walk through it. 'If you take a seat in the waiting room, Katy and I will just have a chat and we'll be with you shortly.'

Anna closed the door firmly and then turned back to her patient. 'Would you have come if it hadn't been for your mother?'

'No.' The girl stared at her. 'There's nothing wrong with me. I'm perfectly healthy. Mum's just a nag.'

Anna sat back down and started to talk to Katy, asking questions about her eating history and questioning her on her attitude to her weight. 'How often do you go to the gym, Katy?'

The girl shrugged. 'Dunno. Most days, I suppose. For about two hours.'

Anna nodded. 'That's quite a lot. It's great to exercise, you're right about that, but we probably need to reduce it slightly and look at your eating patterns.'

She spent some time discussing normal eating, diet and exercise, as well as the physical consequences of an eating disorder.

'I want you to try and eat three meals a day, and would you keep a food diary for me and come and see me again?'

She knew that eating disorders could be extremely difficult to treat but she sensed that in Katy's case the problem was relatively new, which meant that she might be successful in preventing the problem becoming entrenched.

Katy shrugged. 'I suppose so. As long as Mum doesn't come, too. She thinks she understands me.' She rolled her eyes. 'It's tragic.'

Anna suppressed a smile. Far be it from adults to understand teenagers. A sudden inspiration struck. 'Katy, you know everyone in the village...'

The girl shrugged. 'I've lived here all my life,' she said gloomily, 'so I certainly should do.'

'Dr McKenna and I are thinking of setting up a clinic for teenagers, and some input from you as to what would work and what wouldn't would be really helpful.' Anna gave a small smile. 'We'd hate to be seen as "tragic".'

Katy stared at her and a ghost of a smile crossed her face. 'If Dr McKenna is involved, it might be cool.'

Anna ground her teeth. Great. The man was going to be proved right again. If she hadn't been so convinced that the teenage clinic was the right thing for the practice, she might have buried the idea.

As it was, her encounter with Katy made her determined to get the clinic off the ground.

She made a mental note to herself to sort it out at the earliest opportunity and carried on with her surgery.

She'd just seen her third patient when there was a tap on her door and Sam entered.

Her heart skipped in her chest.

Annoyance and another emotion which she chose not to examine made her voice cooler than she'd intended. 'For future reference I'd like to know if you intend to be late for surgery.'

'I took an emergency call this morning. A fact I would have shared with you if you hadn't been so desperate to avoid me.'

'I wasn't desperate.'

He gave a humourless laugh and closed her door firmly behind him. 'Then you're the lucky one. I was so desperate after last night that my body refused to go to sleep.'

Her heart hit her ribcage. 'I don't want to talk about last night.'

'Fine. We'll try it your way to start with. Pretend it didn't happen. If that doesn't work then we'll try it my way. Agreed?'

She stared at him. 'What's your way?'

'We're trying it your way first. When that fails to work, I'll tell you mine.'

Her heat skipped a beat. 'You've got patients piling up outside your surgery, McKenna. You may want to do something about it.'

'In a moment. I'm just checking you're free at lunch-time.'

She glared at him. 'I've already told you, I don't take a lunch-break. And I certainly don't go on dates at lunch-time.'

He strolled across the room, planted both hands on her desk and locked his gaze with hers. 'Firstly, I didn't mention taking a break and, secondly, I didn't say anything about a date.'

'But you—'

'I want to talk to you about Glenda. She has problems we need to help her with. Big problems.'

Anna stared at him. 'Tell me.'

He straightened. 'In case you've forgotten, we've got patients piling up outside the door, Riggs. Let's clear the decks and then we can concentrate on Glenda.'

'She called me this morning in a state.' Sam nursed a coffee, trying not to notice Anna's hair. He loved the sleekness of it. The smoothness. The darkness against her perfect white blouse. It was all he could do to keep his fingers out of it. And away from the rest of her. He just wanted to reach out, grab and help himself. Just as he had the night before.

Damn, he should never have touched her. Then he wouldn't have known that she tasted like a dream.

'A state about what?'

He struggled to keep his mind on the job. 'How much do you know about her mother?'

Anna sat back in her chair. 'Not much, I suppose. Just to say hello to her in passing. She's your father's patient. I don't think she's consulted me at all in the time that I've been here. I only know her as Glenda's mum. You think there's something wrong with her?'

'It would seem so. Glenda rang me this morning because she was afraid to leave her on her own in the house.' Sam ran a hand over his face, trying to keep his mind on the job in hand. Concentration had never been so difficult. 'Basically, she's been trying to ignore the problem. Pretend it isn't happening. But yesterday she lost her mother when they were out shopping.'

'She lost her?'

'She wandered off. Glenda panicked. Apparently that was the final straw that made her call me.'

Anna stared at him. 'You're suggesting that her mother has a form of dementia?'

'I think it's highly probable. We need to refer her to a specialist mental health service for assessment.'

'There's an excellent memory clinic at the hospital.' Anna closed her eyes and breathed out. 'Oh, help. Poor thing. And poor Glenda. What a thing to cope with. And she's an only child, isn't she? No other siblings to help?'

'That's right. And she's really been struggling. Afraid to leave her mother on her own for any length of time, desperate to do her job here and not let us down...'

'She needn't worry about the job,' Anna said immediately. 'We'll make whatever arrangements are necessary to cover her if she needs to be at home, but her job is here for as long as she wants it.'

Sam felt something shift inside him. The woman might be tough on the outside but she was marshmallow on the inside. Loyal and giving. And maybe a part of him had always known that. After all, hadn't she been the one to stay and help his father while he'd chosen a different path? 'It won't be easy.'

'It's Glenda that matters, not the practice. Hannah can do extra time and I'll rack my brains to think of who might be able to help her.' Anna frowned and drummed her fingers on the desk, her neat fingernails tapping a rhythm while she thought. Her brow cleared. 'I know. We'll ask Fiona.'

'She retired a year ago.'

'But she was the most efficient receptionist we ever had and she taught Glenda everything she knew,' Anna reminded him, flicking through a box on her desk and pulling out a card. 'I've got her number here. Once we've spoken to Glenda, we can give her a ring if necessary. But the more important question is how to help Glenda and her mother.'

'I went round there this morning,' Sam told her, a drawn look on his face as he recalled the visit. 'Frankly, I can't begin to imagine how Glenda has coped without help up until now. It's no wonder she's been so stressed. I'm amazed she's been making it to work at all. Her mother was really agitated and aggressive. And she clearly forgets everything, which drives Glenda up the wall.'

Anna groaned. 'I just wish she'd said something sooner. This is all my fault.' She scooped her hair away from her face in a gesture that made him want to groan aloud. 'I should have noticed sooner that something was very wrong. She hasn't been herself for ages. And now I see why. And I see why she's always dashing off at lunch-time and arriving late in the mornings.'

With a determined effort Sam shifted his gaze away from her, trying to remind himself just how badly they clashed. 'She's been checking on her mother—afraid to leave her for too long,' he agreed, 'but don't blame yourself, Riggs. You've been propping up this place virtually single-handed for too long. And that brings us to another subject we're going to have to tackle. You should have told Dad he was no longer up to the job a long time ago.'

Anna bit her lip. 'That isn't true.'

'It's true,' Sam said heavily. 'You've been covering for him, picking up his workload. The sabbatical idea was genius. It enabled you to get some help without telling him outright he needed to retire. Hopefully he'll get the message himself when he's away.'

Her eyes slid away from his. 'Your dad is a brilliant doctor.'

'But his health has been getting worse and you need to be on full power for this job,' Sam said steadily, ignoring the ache inside him. 'It's hard to acknowledge that he's getting old, but that's the truth. There are things Dad should have been doing that he hasn't.'

'That reminds me.' She looked him straight in the eye. 'I want to talk to you about your ideas for that teenage clinic. I want to try it.'

He nodded. 'Good. What changed your mind?'

'I always thought it was a good idea.' Her mouth tilted slightly at the corners and she angled her head. 'It's just that I had to get my head round the fact that it came from you.'

He laughed with appreciation. 'Well, that's honest.'

'I had a girl in here this morning…'

He listened while she told him about Katy and about her plan to involve some of the teenagers in setting up the clinic. It was a great idea.

'I have to hand it to you, Riggs, when you go with an idea, you don't hang around.'

'Now's the time to get them,' she said briskly. 'Long, hot summer evenings are the time when they get carried away. A significant number of our teenage mothers give birth in March.'

'So let's get started. Set up your meeting. What's the problem?'

She breathed in and looked slightly pink. 'You have to be there. Apparently you're "cool".'

He grinned. 'And doesn't that just bug you, Riggs?'

'Actually, no.' She sat back in her chair and surveyed him with those amazing brown eyes. 'If you get the teenagers here, I don't care what tactics you employ. Use your movie-star status if it helps.'

He smiled. 'Any time you want my autograph, Riggs…'

'I'll try and survive without it. But let's get on with this clinic.'

'I thought you hated change.'

'Only when it's done for the sake of change. I can see the benefit of the clinic.'

'My father couldn't. It's one of the reasons I know he should retire. He's stopped seeing what his patients need.'

He saw her eyes cloud, saw the evidence of her very real affection for his father.

'I don't want him to retire.' Anna's chin lifted. 'Changing a few clinics won't matter to him. We can explain why we did it. Things are still the same in the practice.'

'Things never stay the same,' Sam said flatly, rising to his feet in a fluid movement.

'Time moves on and we need to move with it. Let's get through the summer and then we'll sort out what the practice needs, what Dad needs...' He hesitated. 'And what you need.'

He saw her stiffen defensively. 'What do you mean, what I need? I don't need anything.'

He gave a slow smile and watched with satisfaction while her colour rose. 'No? Then it must be just me. Catch you later, Riggs.'

He left the room, ignoring the throb in his loins and the kick of his heart. Who would have thought it? Usually he liked his women gentle and compliant. Everything that Anna wasn't. Anna was stubborn and had a tongue like a whiplash, but he respected her. And that respect was growing, the more he saw of her.

And the fact that the chemistry between them so clearly didn't fit into her plans made the situation even more interesting.

CHAPTER SIX

'MUM'S got an appointment at the memory clinic.' Glenda dropped her bag and removed her cardigan. 'I never thought it would be that quick.'

Aware that Sam had pulled several strings and had had several conversations with the consultant over the past week, Anna merely smiled. 'I'm pleased. When is it?'

'End of the week.' Glenda pulled a face and settled in her chair behind Reception. 'Do you mind if I take a few hours off in the afternoon to go with her?'

'Of course not.' Anna put down the pile of journals she was carrying. 'I wish you'd told me about your mum sooner, Glenda. I feel dreadful, knowing that you were struggling with that on your own.'

Glenda fiddled with her hair. 'Well, to be honest, I don't think I was willing to admit it even to myself.' She flicked on the computer and gave Anna a rueful smile. 'These things happen to other people, don't they? For ages I managed to convince myself she was just a bit forgetful, a bit crotchety. I didn't want to admit it might be anything worse. But lately she's been dreadful. Can't remember a thing.'

'There are things you can do that might help with that.' Anna sat down on the corner of the desk. 'Like keeping everything in the same place and having a routine. Put telephone numbers by the phone and label cupboards to help her remember where things live in the house. I've got a leaflet somewhere with practical tips—I'll look it out for you although I'm sure the clinic will be able to give you something, too.'

Glenda buried her face in her hands. 'I just don't want her to have to go into a home.

But I know that I can't carry on like this either, and that makes me feel so selfish.'

'You're not selfish, Glenda,' Anna said quietly, 'and it's about finding a compromise that works for both of you. Why don't you stop worrying about it until after the appointment? The consultant will be able to assess your mother properly and give you some idea of the future and the options available.'

Glenda nodded and breathed out heavily. 'I suppose that's good advice. It's just that your mind keeps running forward. What if she just can't manage at home any more? What if she isn't safe? To be honest, every morning when I leave the house I wonder whether she's going to have burned it down by the time I come home. It's a nightmare.'

'Well, there are definitely practical things you can do to at least help in that department,' Anna reminded her. 'You can get safety devices installed—gas detectors, smoke alarms, that sort of thing.'

Glenda nodded. 'I know.' She sighed. 'I suppose admitting there's a problem is the first step to doing something about it. At least now it's out in the open.' She looked at Anna and her eyes filled. 'I was so afraid that I'd lose my job.'

'You're part of the practice, Glenda,' Anna said gruffly, leaning forward and giving the older woman a hug. 'You belong here and we'll work through this together. You'll never lose your job.'

Glenda scrubbed her palm across her face and sniffed loudly. 'Don't be kind to me. It makes it worse. But you're such a lovely girl. And your dad would have been so proud of you.'

'It's going to be OK, Glenda,' Anna said softly. 'We'll work something out. Somehow we'll get you whatever help you need.'

The issue of Glenda and her mother occupied Anna's mind for the next few days, and she managed to do a reasonable job of avoiding

Sam. As usual, she ate lunch on the run and in the evening she headed for the beach and jogged along the sand, returning just late enough to avoid the possibility of sharing dinner. She didn't want to sit down opposite Sam again. Didn't want to risk feeling something that she didn't want to feel. *Something complicated.*

All in all, she was doing fine. Life was back to normal.

It was just a shame she couldn't get that kiss out of her mind, she thought crossly as she pushed open the door of the surgery first thing one morning.

It was just because it had been so unexpected, she consoled herself. They'd had a nice evening—she frowned as she remembered it, *an unusually nice evening*—and they'd both just got a bit carried away. Weren't emotions always more intense at night-time? If they kissed during the day they probably wouldn't feel anything at all. Nothing.

When she walked into Reception, Glenda was already at her desk, looking more relaxed than she had in weeks.

'How did it go? I tried to call you last night.' Anna knew Glenda had taken her mother to the hospital the day before but when she'd tried to phone there'd been no answer.

Glenda blushed slightly. 'Actually, after we got back from the hospital, I went for a drink with a friend. I needed to relax and Mum seemed fine so I popped out.'

Anna hid her curiosity, even though she was dying to ask whether the 'friend' was male or female. Privately she hoped it was male. Glenda needed someone to brighten up her life. 'So what did the hospital say?'

'They were really positive and helpful, actually,' Glenda admitted, brushing her hair away from her face. 'And they had lots of amazingly practical suggestions. Like looking for things that trigger her aggressive behaviour. When I talked about it with them, I realised that she gets really, really angry just before she goes to the toilet. So now I know that I need to watch for that and make sure that she gets to the toilet. Who would have thought it could have been brought on by something as simple as that?'

Anna nodded. 'What else?'

'Well, they've got this great day centre where she can go and get involved in all sorts of activities. They do things like art and music therapy. Apparently it gives patients a sense of achievement and that helps to ease some of the frustration.'

'And it means that you can relax, knowing that she's in safe hands.' Anna was relieved that Glenda had been offered some help and support.

Glenda nodded. 'And you were right about them giving me lots of practical tips. They're going to send a nurse round to assess the home, but they've said that it's important to minimise clutter. Apparently that should help to reduce Mum's agitation.'

Anna grinned. 'Hope they never come and look at my house. I invented clutter.'

'And I can vouch for that.' Sam strolled up, smothering a yawn. He looked as though he hadn't been sleeping properly. 'Living with you, Riggs, is a bit like being in a permanent car boot sale. It's a good job your house purchase fell through. You and your belongings never would have fitted into old Jack Lawson's place on the beach. If it didn't already suffer from subsidence, it would have done the minute you moved in. No building could stand the weight of your belongings.'

Anna scowled at him. 'And you're so domesticated and tidy, of course.'

Sam smiled and winked at Glenda. 'At least I can cook.'

'I can cook.' Anna put her hands on her hips and her eyes flashed. How could she have wanted to kiss him? All she wanted to do at the moment was punch him for being so smug and infuriating. 'It's just I don't choose to spend my time slaving over a hot stove for something that vanishes within seconds of being put on the table. It's the ultimate waste of time.'

'What you do to food can't be described as cooking. Is that for me, Glenda?' Sam leaned across the reception desk and picked up his post. 'By the way, we're filming the emergency clinic this morning. And then this afternoon I'm doing a piece to camera on the beach.'

'Will you be wearing your wet suit and carrying a surfboard?' Anna's tone dripped sarcasm and he gave her a solemn look, one that he often used for the camera when he was addressing a serious topic.

'No, I'm doing my caring, responsible doctor bit.' Then he grinned and walked towards his father's consulting room.

Glenda watched him go. 'He's amazing, isn't he? Do you know that he spent the whole of yesterday evening installing gadgets in my house?'

Anna stared at her. 'Gadgets?'

'Yes.' Glenda nodded and ticked them off on her fingers. 'Smoke alarm, some fancy gas thing—and an alarm for Mum. And he shifted some furniture for me. He's incredibly strong.'

Anna inhaled sharply. She didn't want to think about Sam's muscles. It brought back memories of his body pressed hard against hers. *Memories she was trying extremely hard to forget.*

She was still trying not to think about his muscles when Hilda Wakeman hurried in, carrying a large bag.

'Hello, Hilda.' Anna's face brightened. Hilda ran the upmarket delicatessen on the quay and Anna was her most frequent customer. 'How's business?'

'Brisk. I've been up since four-thirty, baking and cooking. It's the only way to keep up with demand. I think tourists eat more than they used to.' Hilda put the bags down. 'Is Dr McKenna around?'

'Just gone into surgery to catch up on some phone calls.' Glenda reached for the phone. 'I'll buzz him for you.'

'No need to bother him. Just wanted to say thank you, that's all.' Hilda gave Anna a rueful smile. 'He did me a good turn yesterday and I always repay a favour.'

It appeared that Sam had done everyone a good turn yesterday, Anna reflected. For a man who professed not to enjoy harbour life, he seemed to have thrown himself back into the community with a commendable amount of dedication.

But it wasn't permanent, she reminded herself.

He was just playing at being a semi-rural GP. He'd be back to the bright lights and the glamour as soon as the summer was over and his father was back.

Sam walked out of his surgery, his face brightening when he saw Hilda. 'My favourite cook!' His eyes narrowed. 'No more problems since yesterday?'

'None.' Hilda smiled warmly. 'Thank goodness you were there.' She turned to Anna. 'Little Nancy, who works for me, cut her finger really badly. Fortunately Sam was passing and brought her up here and did the honours.'

'She needed a couple of stitches. It was a nasty cut. Is she feeling all right today?'

'I've got her working the till and taking it quietly. I did tell her to stay at home but, knowing how busy we are at the moment, she wouldn't hear of it. She's a good girl.' Hilda picked up the bags. 'Now, knowing that you're living with Dr Riggs at the moment, I'm guessing you won't be eating that well, so I've got some things for you here, Dr McKenna, so that you don't have to worry about cooking tonight.'

Anna gritted her teeth. One of the drawbacks of living in a small village was that everyone knew everything about everyone else. Including the fact that she loathed cooking. 'He isn't living *with* me, Hilda—'

'Well, you're sharing a house, which amounts to the same thing,' Hilda said briskly, peering into the bag to remind herself of the contents. 'Marinaded olives, a delicious aubergine salad that the two of you can have as a starter, and—'

'The two of us?' Sam strolled towards her and hooked a finger into the bag. 'Looks fantastic, Hilda. But who are you planning to feed?'

'Well, you and Dr Riggs, of course. Stuck up there in that house on your own and both of you too busy to turn round, let alone cook.' Hilda smacked the back of his hand sharply. 'Don't poke the food. It needs to go straight in the fridge in this heat otherwise you'll be poisoned and blaming me. I've got my reputation to think of.'

Ignoring her stern expression, Sam peered into the bag and sniffed. 'Smells fantastic. I think your reputation as the area's best cook is still intact, Hilda.'

Glenda stood up, her eyes twinkling with amusement. 'Why don't I pop all that in the fridge in the kitchen and you can take it home when you go? Dr Riggs will be delighted. She hates cooking, as you know, Hilda.'

'Of course I know,' Hilda said comfortably. 'It's the reason she stops by almost every night and picks up something for her dinner. But I thought I'd save you the trouble tonight. And I thought I'd make something a bit special by way of a thank you. There's a lovely seafood pie and fresh apple crumble with clotted cream.'

Anna grunted, torn between pleasure at the anticipation of one of Hilda's dinners and irritation at the fact that everyone was discussing her lack of culinary skills so freely. 'I don't know why everyone is so obsessed with the fact that I don't cook. Does a woman always have to cook?'

'Not when they have a deli like mine in the village,' Hilda said calmly, handing the last of the bags to Glenda to store in the fridge. 'And my Geoff popped an excellent bottle of white in the bag, too. A sauvignon blanc, that's his personal favourite. And I added a lovely scented candle. Have a good evening.'

With that she winked at them both and hurried back to her car.

'Scented candle?' Sam stared after her. 'What the hell was that all about? Give me the wine and the food, definitely, but what's with the scented candle?'

Anna scowled and raked her hair out of her eyes. 'You heard. She knows I can't cook and she thinks I'm starving you. Although why I'm supposed to be responsible for the contents of your stomach, goodness knows. And I haven't got a clue about the scented candle. Perhaps it's to keep wasps away.'

'Nothing to do with wasps. She's matchmaking,' Glenda said calmly, fishing in the bag and removing the candle. 'Oh, look—it's one of those special ones set in driftwood.

It's so pretty. It'll look lovely on that table on your deck. How romantic.'

She put it carefully back in the bag and Anna felt her colour rise. 'Romantic? Matchmaking?'

Glenda smiled and stowed the bag carefully behind Reception. 'Of course. The whole village is hoping that the two of you will fall in love and set up shop together. It would be a fairy-tale ending.'

There was a pulsing silence.

For a moment Anna stood still, totally speechless. Then her temper exploded. 'Since when did fairy tales come with loud arguments and the threat of physical injury?' She whirled round and glared at Sam. 'Don't just stand there laughing! Say something!'

Sam ran a hand over his face but his blue eyes gleamed with humour. 'Looks like I don't have to cook dinner tonight.'

Anna all but stamped her foot. 'How can you be so calm? They think you're going to stay, McKenna. Step into your father's

place.' She bit her lip. 'They're trying to…
They want us to…' She couldn't even bring
herself to voice the idea, it was so ridiculous.

'Get together,' Sam finished for her helpfully, his gaze disconcertingly direct. 'They
just want a doctor they know. You can't
blame them for that. And matchmaking goes
on all the time in villages.'

'Between people who like each other,
McKenna,' Anna reminded him tartly. 'We
don't like each other.'

He looked at her thoughtfully. 'No, that's
right. We don't, do we?'

Something in his tone made her remember
the kiss and she blushed. 'Well, finally we
agree on something. I haven't got time to
stand around here all day, talking about village gossip. I've got work to do.'

'Me, too.'

Glenda glanced between them and sighed.
'Well, if the two of you are arguing too much
to eat Hilda's food, give me a call and I'll
come and eat it.'

*   *   *

'You're seriously going to sit down and eat dinner with the whole harbour watching?'

His eyes flickered along the bay. 'You're paranoid. I don't see anyone showing any interest in us.'

She grunted and swept her hair back from her face. 'That's because you're used to living in London and you automatically assume that no one is interested in you. Here, everyone is interested in you. You should remember that. Somewhere out there someone probably has a telescope fixed on this deck and they're watching our every move. Light that candle and we may as well book the church.'

'Your wrong, actually. In my job it's like being in a goldfish bowl. But, frankly, I don't care who's watching. There's no way I'm wasting this food.' Sam put a loaded plate in the middle of the table. 'You can go and eat baked beans in your bedroom if you prefer. I won't tell anyone.'

Anna stared at the aubergine salad and felt her mouth water. 'You'll never eat all that by yourself.'

'Never underestimate my appetites,' he drawled, a wicked glint in his eyes as he surveyed her. 'And I should probably point out that if you carry on being this jumpy around me, the village is going to be gossiping even more than it is at the moment.'

'I'm not jumpy.'

One dark eyebrow lifted. 'Riggs, you're like a kangaroo. The moment I enter a room, you bounce out of it. This is as good a time as any to ask you why.'

She glared at him. 'Don't flatter yourself it has anything to do with you. I'm a busy woman. Lots to do.'

'If you say so.' With smooth, measured movements he finished laying the table. 'I'm just warning you how it might look from the outside. And don't be embarrassed. I'm avoiding you, too.'

'You are?'

'That's right. It's the only way I can concentrate and get any work done. Now, are you eating or not? The seafood pie is heating in the oven so we need to get started.'

Anna stared at him.

He was having trouble concentrating?

He was thinking about her? Suddenly she felt unsettled and she wasn't used to feeling unsettled. She was used to knowing where her life was going. To being in control. Around Sam McKenna, she didn't feel in control at all.

Her brain told her to leave but her taste buds had other ideas. 'All right, we'll share the meal. But we'll live to regret it. I'm willing to bet that someone is watching.'

'Let them watch.' Sam sprawled in a chair and lifted his beer, his eyes resting on the surf.

'You used to hate all that. The fact that everyone knew everything about you,' she reminded him, picking at an olive. 'It was one of the reasons you couldn't wait to go to London. You wanted to be anonymous.' She laughed as she realised what she'd said. 'Not that you're exactly anonymous, Dr Hotshot.'

His eyes swivelled to hers. 'I'm just a normal, everyday kind of guy.'

'I hate to disillusion you, but you've never been normal, McKenna.' She took another olive, admired its shiny blackness before popping it into her mouth. 'Arrogant, self-assured and wrong about virtually everything. Never normal. These olives are good. What exactly does Hilda do to them?'

'No idea, but they're always sold by lunch-time so it must be something special. How long has my dad been struggling?'

The swift change of subject threw her, just as he'd known it would. 'Most of last winter,' she admitted finally, dropping an olive stone onto her empty plate. 'He had a chest infection in October that he just couldn't throw off. After that he just seemed to slow down. I kept hoping he'd pick up but he never did.'

'Damn.' Sam stretched long legs in front of him. 'I can't believe I didn't notice. He just seemed the same to me.'

Anna stared across the beach. 'That's the strange thing about parents. You see them the way you think they are—the way they've always been—rather than the way they really are. I remember it took me ages to realise how ill Dad was. To me he was just Dad. And then I came home from university one holiday and for a moment I saw him as other people must see him. And I realised he'd aged. And lost weight. And grown old somewhere along the way. I just hadn't noticed.'

She felt a wave of emotion swamp her and blinked several times to clear her vision. No matter how much time passed, she still missed her parents.

'I remember that time. You walked around the whole holiday looking like a ghost.' Sam watched her across the table. 'That was a hard time for you, losing your dad and your mum so close together.'

'Neither of them would have been any good without the other, so it was probably for the best,' Anna said gruffly, turning her attention back to her plate, 'and I got through. Your parents were brilliant.'

'You've always been the daughter they never had.'

Their gazes locked and Anna's eyes narrowed as a thought entered her head. 'McKenna, you don't think— I mean, they wouldn't...'

He didn't pretend to misunderstand her. 'They're as capable of matchmaking as everyone else in the village, so I suppose it's possible.'

She put her fork down with a clatter. 'But they know us so well. They know that we clash, that we drive each other nuts—that we just couldn't—'

'Couldn't we?' He reached for the pepper, a strange light in his eyes as he glanced towards her. 'Just as well they didn't see that kiss the other night.'

Her heart hammered her ribcage. 'We agreed not to talk about that.'

'Your rules, Riggs. I'm willing to talk about it any time you like. And go for a repeat performance.'

Her pulse jumped and she took some sensible breaths. 'That would be ridiculous.'

'Would it? Why?'

'Because we are completely and totally wrong for each other,' she snapped, 'and that kiss was a mistake.'

'You didn't enjoy it?'

'What do you want me to say?' She glared at him. 'That you're good at kissing? Yes, you're good at kissing. Yes, I enjoyed it. But it wasn't real.'

'Felt real enough to me.'

'Look, McKenna...' She took a deep breath and struggled with her patience and the rush of unfamiliar feelings inside her. 'We'd managed to get through a whole evening without killing each other, I'd drunk champagne, which always goes to my head, the atmosphere was gooey, it was dark...'

She ladled on the excuses and he studied her carefully.

'You want me to kiss you in daylight when you're sober, just to test that theory?'

'You're being deliberately annoying.' She stood up and picked up the empty plate. 'I'll get the seafood pie.'

Of course she didn't want him to test the theory.

She didn't want him to touch her again.

It was just too confusing.

She didn't like the man. He drove her nuts. Always had done, always would do. And just because he knew how to kiss a woman into a coma, it didn't change that fact.

The situation grew more tense every day.

It seemed that the more she tried to avoid him, the more their paths crossed. And wherever they were, Polly seemed to be filming.

They had a meeting with a group of local teenagers and talked about how they could improve the health provision in the area. It was a lively, stimulating evening and it served to confirm to Anna that Sam had been right to suggest the idea. A teenage health clinic would work really well as long as they listened carefully to what was needed. The teenagers themselves, led by Katy, brainstormed ideas and decided to design the posters themselves.

'I just love it when someone else does all the work.' Sam leaned back in his chair and smiled at them. 'Just as long as people know that this is an open clinic. No appointments needed. Anyone under the age of eighteen can just turn up and hang out. You can see the doctor, talk to the nurse or just mingle. And every week one of us will give a short talk.'

'Can we talk about confidentiality?' One of the younger girls bit her lip and went pink. 'I mean, what you have to tell our parents and what can just be between us?'

Sam nodded, his expression serious. 'Of course. Good topic. Add that to the list, Katy.'

Katy scribbled away and by the end of the session they'd produced a long list of topics and general ideas for the clinic.

'We'll put a poster up in the surf shop, that's where most of the teenagers hang out,' Katy said, making a few deft strokes with her pen and lifting up her pad. 'What do you think of something like this for the design?'

Anna blinked. 'Katy, it's brilliant.'

Katy flushed. 'I'm doing art at college. I love drawing. I can make it better than this. I'll do it on the computer at home.'

By the time they'd finished, they'd planned their clinic down to the last detail.

'Go on.' Sam turned to her as they locked up at the end of the evening. 'Tell me I was right.'

'It's a good idea,' Anna conceded, dropping the keys into her bag. 'It remains to be seen if it will work.'

'It will work. Katy was really joining in. Are you still seeing her?'

Anna nodded, pausing by her car. 'She keeps a food diary and we talk about it and she's cut down on her exercise. I think she's acknowledging that she has a problem, which is good.'

'Unusual for someone with an eating disorder,' Sam observed, juggling his keys in the palm of his hand.

'Fortunately, I think Katy has only just developed a problem,' Anna said. 'It was a boy that she went out with. Kept telling her she was fat.'

Sam rolled his eyes. 'Teenage boys. Perhaps we ought to do something about body image in our clinic.'

'Good idea.'

He grinned. 'Careful, Riggs. We're agreeing on rather a lot at the moment.'

'Nonsense.' Suddenly flustered, she tugged open her car door and tossed her bag on the seat. The way he was looking at her made her feel hot. Aware of herself. So full of frustrated desire that her whole body felt ready to explode.

She'd never felt like this before. Never wanted a man so badly.

Especially one that she didn't even like. It just didn't make sense.

It was that kiss, she decided crossly, sliding into her car and slamming her car door shut. If they hadn't shared that stupid kiss then none of this would have happened. She could have carried on being irritated by him, finding him infuriating and aggravating. And she could have slept at night.

As it was, she hadn't slept properly for ages and the tension between them was building to almost intolerable levels.

Every time they were in a room together the atmosphere sizzled and thrummed and Anna was reaching screaming pitch.

She'd tried to bury sexual frustration in work, concentrating on her patients, helping Glenda, catching up with all the things that she'd been too busy to do with David ill. But none of it worked.

They carried on for a few more days and in the end Sam took control, grabbing Anna by the arm and hauling her into the nearest consulting room.

He closed the door firmly and pushed her against it, one arm planted either side of her head. 'OK, Riggs, we've tried it your way and it isn't working.'

'What do you mean, it isn't working?'

'You said that if we both ignored it and pretended that it never happened, it would go away.' He stepped closer to her, pressing her against the door. 'It hasn't gone away, Riggs. It's still there.'

She placed her hands on his chest and struggled to breathe.

'I don't know what you mean—' She didn't even finish the sentence before his mouth came down on hers and he showed her exactly what he meant.

The explosion was instant.

Fierce hunger exploded inside her and Anna lifted herself on her toes and pressed herself closer, moaning as he explored her mouth with erotic expertise.

She'd never been kissed like this before.

She'd never felt like this before.

She felt the heat build in her body, felt the powerful throb of his arousal against her and the urgency of his mouth on hers.

Completely forgetting where they were, she gave herself up to sensation. Eyes closed, she breathed in the masculine scent of him, felt the strength and purpose of his hands as he touched her but most of all revelled in the skilled possession of his mouth as he kissed her.

It was only when she felt the cool air brush her exposed breasts that she realised that he'd undone her blouse.

Shocked by how fast things had moved, she placed her hands in the centre of his chest. 'We've got to stop doing this.' She groaned the words against his mouth and he lifted his head just enough to respond.

'Or we could carry on.'

'We can't do that.'

'Why not?' His voice was husky and his eyes roved over her flushed face, revealing a considerable degree of masculine satisfaction.

'Because sex would complicate things.'

'We're both single people.' He bent his head and kissed her neck, his touch warm and seductive. 'Who are we hurting?'

She couldn't reason or concentrate when he was this close. She just knew it wasn't what she had planned for herself.

She wasn't ready for a relationship. At least, not yet. And when she was ready it wouldn't be with a wickedly dangerous man like Sam McKenna. They clashed. They never agreed on anything. He irritated her beyond belief.

But he knew how to kiss and he had the most incredible hands…

She tried to talk sense into herself and failed, mostly because his mouth was still busy seducing hers. She moaned and kissed him back. Did it really matter if they weren't exactly well matched? If they were totally unsuited in every way except physically? Why shouldn't they just have some fun? As he had rightly pointed out, who would they be hurting?

CHAPTER SEVEN

SAM stood on the beach and tried to concentrate on what he was supposed to be saying.

James, the sound man, was making various adjustments and Polly was talking to the cameraman. In a moment he was going to have to start talking about holiday health and all he could think about was Anna.

He ran a hand over the back of his neck and the make-up girl sprinted forward with her box of tricks.

'Standing in the sun for too long is making you sweat.'

Sam surrendered to her ministrations and chose not to enlighten her. It wasn't the sun that was making him sweat. It was thoughts of Anna. Her fabulous legs. Her amazing hair. The way her mouth and skin tasted. It came as a considerable shock to discover that

Anna had the ability to seriously disturb his equilibrium. Who would have thought it?

'OK, Sam, we're ready.' Polly walked towards him. 'We're going to use some shots of families on the beach doing normal things and then we'll have you talking about sun protection. Are you ready?'

Sam nodded. As ready as he'd ever be.

The afternoon passed quickly while they filmed various shots and they were just finishing for the day, Polly finally satisfied, when there were shouts from the cliffs behind them.

John swung his camera round. 'Someone in trouble up there?'

'Not up there.' Polly caught Sam's arm and pointed. 'Out there.'

He followed her gaze and saw a small rubber dinghy that had floated out past the rocks. There was one little girl in it and she was crying and waving. The sea was rough, the waves crashing around her and threatening to swamp the tiny dinghy. 'Oh, hell, this beach is covered in warnings about the currents and the waves. Why do people ignore them?'

Even as he started sprinting towards the sea, he could hear the screaming, see the sudden surge of people as they sensed drama and danger and moved in to watch.

'Get the people away, Poll,' he yelled, 'and call the coastguard.'

He dragged off his shirt as he ran, trying to identify the family of the little girl in the dinghy. 'Do you know her?' He sprinted past people, barking the question until finally he found the parents at the edge of the waves.

The father was frantically wading into the water towards his daughter.

'I'll get her.' Sam pulled him back and the man gripped his arm hard, panic visible in his eyes as he explained what had happened.

'It's not just her. My teenage son was in that dinghy. He's fallen into the water—he's not that great a swimmer.'

'Stay here.' Sam waded into the water and then turned as someone sprinted up beside him.

It was Anna. Slender and poised in a black swimsuit, her gaze grimly determined. She didn't waste time with words, just handed him a buoyancy aid and kept one for herself. He noticed that she was also carrying a life-jacket.

'Let's go.'

He didn't argue, pleased to have her help. Anna was a first-class swimmer and he knew she had a life-saving certificate.

She dived into the waves with the skill of a dolphin, her strong overarm stroke powering her through the water towards the stricken dinghy. He followed swiftly, overtook her and reached the little girl first.

'He fell in.' The girl was hysterical, clinging to the edges of the tiny inflatable boat, which rocked precariously in the rough sea. It seemed ridiculously insubstantial. 'He was being stupid, playing around, and then he fell in.'

Anna surfaced next to Sam and swam around to the girl, one hand on the dinghy. 'Try not to panic. We'll find your brother. What's your name?'

The girl choked on a sob. 'Lottie—'

'Well, Lottie—' Anna broke off and gave a gasp and a splutter as a wave broke over her head, almost swamping her and the tiny boat. Relieved that she was such a strong swimmer, Sam watched as she surfaced immediately and shook her head clear of the water. 'Lottie, we're going to get you somewhere safe.' Her lashes were clumped together with seawater and she swept a hand across her face to clear her vision. 'I want you to sit still in that boat of yours and hold on very tightly while we work out the best way to do this.'

Her dark hair plastered to her head, as sleek as an otter, she kicked her legs fiercely and looked at Sam.

'This thing is going to capsize,' he said, scraping the water out of his eyes and treading water himself while he marshalled his thoughts. The sea was becoming rougher by the minute and he knew that the dinghy wasn't going to offer protection for long. 'Get a life-jacket on her while I see if I can find her brother.'

She didn't argue with him.

'Lottie, I want you to put your arms in this and then we're going to zip it up.' Anna struggled as another huge wave hit them. She paused for a moment, waited for a lull and then helped the girl into the life-jacket. When she'd finished she turned and looked around her and realised Sam was gone.

For a moment her heart jerked with panic and then she realised that he must have dived down under the water.

Another wave crashed down on her and this time the dinghy was totally submerged. Relieved that she'd got the life-jacket on the girl in time, Anna kicked strongly and held the child above the water, trying to calm her each time a wave swamped them, her eyes flitting around frantically for signs of Sam.

He'd been under too long.

Out of the corner of her eye she saw the lifeboat arrive, but all she cared about now was Sam. Damn, he shouldn't have dived. It was too much of a risk. The waves were too rough, the tide was too strong…

And then he surfaced, right next to her, gasping for air, struggling to keep another body afloat.

'You got him.'

'He must have hit his head on a rock. But he's been under for a while.' Sam's breathing was jerky as he gasped for air. Water clung to his lashes and the rough stubble of his jaw as he carefully held the teenage boy's face above the water. 'We need to get him out of here, fast.'

The lifeboat crew, practised in rescues such as these, swung into action and Anna gladly relinquished the little girl into their capable hands before turning her attention to helping Sam.

'We need to keep him flat—you know that. He has to be lifted out of the water in a prone position or we risk circulatory collapse.'

'I know.'

'And we need to watch his neck.' Sam yelled instructions to the lifeboat crew, who were preparing to lift the teenager out of the water.

Through her watery vision, Anna spotted John Craddock at the helm.

There was a clack-clacking sound overhead and the rescue helicopter arrived.

'Thank goodness,' Anna shouted, gasping as another wave broke over her head. 'They can fly him straight to hospital. Are you OK?'

'Never better.' Sam managed a wry grin. 'Apart from the gallon of seawater I've swallowed.'

Finally the rescue was completed and Sam and Anna swam back to the shore, both of them cold and exhausted.

'Have the parents gone?' Sam accepted a towel gratefully from a bystander and wiped his face.

'Someone gave them a lift to the hospital.' Polly was standing next to him with the rest of the crew. 'Well, I have to say, you two, you know how to give the viewers something exciting to watch. That was amazing.'

Anna twisted her long hair round her hand and squeezed until water dripped onto the sand. 'You were filming that?'

'Every minute.' Polly smiled and shielded her eyes against the sun. 'Not just for our documentary—although for holiday health I think that was a pretty powerful message— but for the news as well.'

Anna rubbed her hand over her face to clear her vision. 'I can't believe you filmed it.'

'It's my job.' Polly handed her another towel. 'Just as this is your job. Sort of.' She pulled a face. 'Actually, I don't think it is your job to plunge into crashing waves and a cold sea to rescue someone who shouldn't have been out in a dinghy anyway. People should think before they act. Now do you see the point of our programme?'

Anna shivered despite the towel and the warmth of the sun. 'I suppose if it stops someone taking blow-up craft into rough waves, yes.' She rubbed her skin with the towel but her teeth continued to chatter.

'For the record, the two of you were amazing.' Polly glanced at the cameraman. 'We got it all, didn't we? Every adrenaline-pumping minute?'

'Oh, yes.' He grinned and tapped the camera. 'I wasn't missing that. I even got the frantic look on Anna's face when she thought Sam wasn't coming up again.'

Oh, hell.

Anna huddled inside the towel. 'I was just worried about running the practice single-handed,' she muttered, and Polly smiled.

'Of course you were. The funny thing about you two is that you disagree violently on everything that doesn't matter, but when it comes to something important you don't even have to communicate. You just anticipate the other's needs. Just like that time in the surgery with little Lucy. Maybe when you see the footage, you'll see what I mean.'

'Something's making me feel sick, Polly,' Anna said, her teeth still chattering, 'and it's either the seawater I've swallowed or it could possibly be the rubbish you're spouting.'

'Deny it all you like,' Polly said airily, 'but the two of you work well together. And on camera you make magic. This programme is going to be a hit. And you're going to be a hit, Anna. You'd better get yourself an agent.'

She turned away to say something to the sound man and Sam stepped forward with a wicked grin.

'Any time you want to make magic with me, Riggs, just say the word.'

Anna glared at him and opened her mouth to say something sharp, but Polly turned her attention back to them before she could speak.

'Can the two of you explain a little bit about what you were trying to do in that rescue? In relatively simple language, of course.'

Anna smiled helpfully. 'Save someone from drowning?'

Polly ignored her and looked at Sam. 'I thought the two of you could have a conversation about it—you know, something natural but informative.'

He nodded, instantly professional. 'Sure, Polly. Let's just ad lib and see what we get.' He dropped the towel and turned to Anna, water still clinging to his lashes, like some sort of god who had just emerged from the sea. 'Of course, there have been some extraordinary examples of survival after long periods of submersion in ice-cold water—'

'We could experiment if you like.' Anna tilted her head to one side and smiled at him, her wet hair sliding over her bare shoulders.

'I could hold you under ice-cold water and we could see what happens.'

There was a snort of laughter from the sound man.

'Cut!' Polly shook her head and laughed. 'That wasn't exactly what I had in mind, Anna!'

Anna's gaze was locked on Sam's.

Something dangerous gleamed in his eyes. 'On reflection, holding me under ice-cold water isn't a bad idea,' he muttered, taking a step towards her. 'It might be the only solution if we carry on with your plan.'

Aware that the crew was listening, Anna felt her cheeks heat and backed away from him.

'OK, let's try this thoroughly staged and unnatural conversation you want,' she said quickly, suddenly wanting to distract Sam from coming towards her. Had he forgotten that they were being filmed, for goodness' sake? 'Dr McKenna...' She kept her voice brisk and professional. 'It's important to remember that cold can protect lives as well as endanger them.'

This time she played it straight, as they'd requested, talking with Sam about the management of near drowning, using terms that a layman would understand.

Finally Polly was satisfied. 'Fantastic. You two are going to be our star turn. And, Anna, I love your swimming costume.'

Anna stared down at herself in amazement. 'It's just a costume.'

'It looks great.' The sound man scratched the side of his nose and gave her a cheeky grin. 'I think we can guarantee a male audience for this particular series.'

Anna's mouth fell open. 'You're saying that people are going to watch this because they like my swimming costume?'

'No, although that helps. They'll watch because you're beautiful and full of guts,' Polly said bluntly, 'and because there's enough spark between the two of you to start a forest fire.'

'Oh, not that again,' Anna snapped, scooping her damp hair over one shoulder and deciding that enough was enough. 'If we've finished here, I'm off. I need to warm up after my impromptu dip.'

She sprinted back along the sand towards the house, trying to outrun her feelings. It didn't work.

She slowed to a walk and gave a groan.

No matter how hard she tried, she couldn't stop thinking about Sam. And it was getting worse by the minute.

Damn.

She took the steps that led from the beach to the deck of the house and padded round to the hot tub.

She flicked the switch, slid into the bubbling water with a moan of pleasure and closed her eyes. This was one of her favourite places. She waited for the tension to seep out of her, but this time she couldn't relax. Couldn't get him out of her mind. And when she heard footsteps on the deck, she knew it was him.

Her eyes flew open and she moved in the water. 'I was just getting out.'

'You only just got in.' He was still dressed in his surf shorts and nothing else. He had an amazing body, strong, powerfully built and immensely fit, and he stood there, legs planted firmly apart, totally unselfconscious.

She, on the other hand, was aware of every male inch of him.

Her throat dried. 'I just wanted to warm up.'

'And how warm are you?' He sat down, swung his legs over the side and slid in next to her, his gaze meshing with hers as he moved in close. 'How warm are you, Riggs?'

She swallowed, trapped by his gaze. 'I'm warming up fast.'

His blue eyes flickered to her mouth. 'Need any help?'

'I think I might,' she managed huskily before his mouth found hers and they both gave in to the greed that had been consuming them both for days.

'Hell, Riggs.' His mouth devoured hers hungrily. 'I love your body.'

'Same here.' She felt their legs tangle, felt his arm haul her close and felt his other hand at her breast. 'Oh, help, we shouldn't do this.'

'Stop saying that.' He groaned the words into her neck. 'We're doing it and that's final.'

'No.' She tilted her head and gasped for air. 'I mean, we shouldn't be doing this here, in public.'

'It's not public.' His tongue tasted her skin. 'This is a private deck. The only way anyone can see is if they're up here with us.'

Her whole body was on fire, her heart leaping in her chest.

'We agreed it was a mistake…'

'We never agree on anything.' His hand cupped her face and his mouth came down on hers again, stifling her cry.

He felt so good. Hard. Strong. Male.

And she wanted him.

She broke away, her breath coming in tiny pants, her fingers digging into his biceps. 'We really ought to discuss this.' She was trying to concentrate but all she could think about was the play of muscle under her fingers and how much she wanted him. 'We shouldn't do this on impulse.' She gasped as his mouth found her throat again. 'We should talk.'

'Talking isn't going to warm either of us up.'

Her eyes closed as she felt the erotic touch of his mouth on hers. She'd thought she'd been kissed before. Dozens of times. But maybe she was wrong because it had never felt like this. No one kissed like Sam McKenna.

She knew that what they were doing wasn't sensible, but it felt too right to even contemplate stopping.

His arm curved around her waist and he pulled her onto his lap. 'Body heat is an important source of warmth in these circumstances, Riggs,' he murmured, his voice deep and unreasonably sexy. 'Important to share what we have.'

Her whole body ached and throbbed and she twisted under the water, bringing herself into closer contact with him, hearing his groan, feeling his immediate response.

'It's time you lost the swimming costume.' His hands skimmed her shoulders, sliding it down, and she gave a strangled moan as she felt his clever, seeking fingers graze her taut nipples.

'McKenna. *Sam!*'

He tugged the costume lower still, his hands sliding over her belly and downwards till she shifted her hips against him, desperate to ease the blinding, greedy ache.

Bringing his mouth back to hers, he kissed her savagely, stoking the fire that flared between them.

It took all her will-power to stop it from going all the way. 'Sam...' She groaned his name, her eyes closed. 'We can't do this. Not here. We should stop now...'

She felt the rise and fall of his chest as he struggled to breathe normally. 'You're probably right. Not here. Are you warmer now? Because that's all I was doing, of course, warming you up.'

She looked at him, her breathing unsteady. 'Just a little warmer. Thanks.'

'My pleasure.'

She was still on his lap, still aware of every masculine inch of him. 'Well... I, er, that was...interesting.'

He ran a hand over his face and made a visible effort to pull himself together. 'It certainly proved a point.'

She could still feel the brush of his hard thigh against hers and her brain was refusing to function. 'What point?'

'That it was nothing to do with the dark, the champagne and the atmosphere.'

She slid her arms back into her costume and moved off his lap. 'We don't like each other, McKenna.'

His eyes followed her every movement. 'We could work on that.'

'We never agree on anything.'

'I'm willing to say yes to you the minute you ask me the right question.'

She stood up, breathlessly aware of his gaze on her body. 'We're going to take a step backwards, McKenna, and try and get a grip on ourselves. We need to stop putting ourselves in the position where this happens. I still think this isn't a good idea.'

It would complicate her life and she didn't need complications.

'Excuse me asking this.' He spread his arms wide along the rim of the hot tub, the muscles in his shoulders bunching. 'But exactly which bit doesn't work for you?'

'The you and I bit.' She flicked her hair away from her face. 'It's just not— Well, it isn't what we do.'

'Why?'

She frowned, but met his gaze head on, never one to avoid an issue just because it was uncomfortable. 'Well, for a start, because it would make things awkward between us.'

'Awkward? What can be more awkward than walking round in a state of permanent arousal, which is what's happening to me at the moment?' The corner of his mouth shifted. 'Riggs, I'm a grown man, not some emotionally stunted teenager. I can make love to you and still have a civilised working relationship, if that's what's bothering you.'

His words had a disturbing effect on her heart rate. 'You're only here for the summer.'

'So?' He shrugged. 'We could have fun. Do you know your problem?'

'I don't have a problem.'

'You plan too much. You need to go with the flow. Live a little. Do something on impulse.'

Impulse.

Anna stared at him. The impulse to dive back into the hot tub with him was almost overwhelming.

She sucked in a breath and pulled herself together. 'It's the ability to reason and think that distinguishes us from animals, McKenna,' she said primly, but there was a definite tremor in her voice and he gave a slow grin that churned up her insides more than ever.

'That must be why you bring out the beast in me.'

'I need to do this my way.'

'Fine. You do whatever you need to do to bring your brain and body in line with mine.' His eyes glittered with serious intent. 'But do it fast, Riggs, before we both burn up.'

Sam stood under a cold shower and wondered if anyone had ever conducted an experiment into the quantity of icy water required to kill a ravenous libido because his was decidedly out of control.

If Anna hadn't stopped him, he would have made love to her in the hot tub and he wouldn't have given a damn if the cameras had been running and the entire village had been watching.

He reached for the shampoo and wondered how long she was going to hold out.

Was she right?

Would it make things awkward between them?

He closed his eyes, let the water rinse the soap from his hair and then reached for a towel, a smile on his face as he contemplated the situation. Things had always been awkward between them. They'd never had a smooth, comfortable relationship. It had always been like walking over rocks in bare feet.

He dried himself, pulled on a pair of clean shorts and stared into the mirror.

Of course, part of him was telling him to run a mile. Anna would be no man's idea of a gentle, compliant partner. She'd be snapping and fighting all the way. He had no doubt that even during sex she'd have an opinion. And she'd probably waste no time in expressing it.

The prospect heated his blood to a dangerous level. The need he felt was so powerful, so all-consuming that he knew it was just a matter of time. It was when, not whether. And he sensed it was the same for her. He doubted that either of them would hold out for long.

CHAPTER EIGHT

'YOU'RE both famous.' Glenda made them both a cup of tea the following morning when they appeared for surgery. 'Your rescue has been shown on every news bulletin since last night. Amazing.'

Anna took the tea with a smile of thanks, carefully avoiding Sam's eye. She'd seen the bulletin and winced at the footage of her and Sam. She'd never realised that her black costume was so revealing.

'They'll incorporate a longer version when the programme goes out,' Sam told Glenda, handing her a pile of papers. 'I ran these off the internet for you. Have a read and see what you think. How's your mother doing today?'

'She's so much better.' Glenda settled herself behind her desk and flicked on the computer. 'I've labelled everything in the sitting-room and put the phone next to her, and I followed your idea of sticking my picture next to the speed dial so that she can remember which button to press if she wants me.'

Anna lifted her head. 'You're full of good ideas, Sam.'

'I certainly am.' His eyes locked with hers. 'You ought to try some of them some time.'

She swallowed. Why was it that she was suddenly so aware of every single inch of him? There'd been a time, not that many days before, when all she'd wanted to do when she'd laid eyes on Sam had been to pick a fight. Now, suddenly, she just wanted to strip him naked.

Glenda reached for the keys. 'I'll unlock that front door if you're ready.'

Sam's eyes didn't leave Anna's. 'I'm ready. How about you?'

She knew what he was asking and suddenly she couldn't speak. Aware that Glenda was staring at her curiously, she licked her lips. 'I think I'm probably ready, too.'

Sam's mouth moved into a smile of raw, masculine satisfaction. 'Glad to hear it, Riggs.'

Glenda frowned at them. 'Is something going on that I don't know about?'

'Nothing.' Anna's voice sounded raspy and she cleared her throat and glanced at her watch. 'We need to get going. We've got a busy day and the beach barbecue tonight.'

Glenda nodded, her eyes sparkling. 'I'm certainly going. I've got a girl staying the night to keep an eye on Mum and I intend to enjoy myself.'

Anna grinned. 'And who with, exactly? Would this be the same ''friend'' you saw the other night?'

Glenda's colour deepened. 'It might be. I presume you're both going?'

Sam suppressed a yawn. 'I'm supposed to be doing a piece to camera about holiday night-life. The perils of enjoying yourself. Too much alcohol and unprotected sex. That type of thing.'

Glenda giggled naughtily. 'I know quite a few people in this village who could star in that.'

Anna gave a reluctant laugh. 'You're both terrible. And, Sam, you should concentrate on the teenagers. You wouldn't believe how many I have in here after parties on the beach. For goodness' sake, talk about safe sex. It's definitely a subject to address in our new clinic.'

Glenda hurried off to open the doors and Sam turned to Anna.

'And when I've finished my piece to camera,' he said softly, 'you and I have some business to sort out, Riggs. And this time we're doing it my way.'

She stared at him, hypnotised by the look in his eyes. 'Your way?'

'Your way hasn't worked and I haven't had an undisturbed night's sleep for weeks.' His eyes dropped to her mouth. 'And it's only fair to warn you that if you're planning to argue then you're going to lose.'

'I wasn't planning to argue.'

'No?' His mouth curved into a sexy smile. 'Now, that is a first.'

Anna spent the entire day in a state of heightened awareness. She went through her surgeries and her calls with only half her mind in action, the other half thinking about Sam and the forthcoming evening.

Why shouldn't they further their relationship? she reasoned.

As he'd rightly pointed out, who were they going to hurt? They were both consenting adults and neither of them was involved with anyone else. They found each other attractive. It was a relatively simple situation.

Except that it didn't feel simple.

It didn't feel simple at all.

Neither did dressing for the beach barbecue. The problem with being a GP in a small, tight-knit community, Anna reflected as she stared at the dress that she'd laid out on her bed, was that you were always in the spotlight and your behaviour had to be above reproach. She could never risk getting drunk in public or making an exhibition of herself.

Did the outfit she'd chosen classify as making an exhibition of herself?

She fingered the fabric gingerly. She'd bought the dress as a joke. To provoke Sam. But things had moved on and now she had a feeling that she'd be provoking a reaction entirely different from the one she'd originally anticipated.

A womanly smile spread across her face and she lifted the dress.

Impulse.

Wasn't that what Sam had said?

Well, this dress had definitely been an impulse buy, purchased after he'd made that comment about her not being sufficiently 'girly'.

And she was going to wear it.

She was wearing hot pink.

Sam felt his tongue almost fall out of his

mouth as Anna walked out of the house onto the deck. Her silky dark hair was caught up on top of her head, her perfect mouth highly glossed. Her legs were long and lightly tanned and the heels she was wearing looked as though they should come with a health warning.

She paused and angled her head. 'Say something, McKenna.'

He swallowed and dragged his eyes away from her legs. 'You don't wear pink, Riggs.'

'Tonight I'm wearing pink.'

He ran a hand over the back of his neck. 'Is it hot tonight, or is it me?'

She gave a slow smile that made his hormones shriek in protest. 'It's hot. That's why I chose to wear a cool dress.'

'There is nothing cool about that dress, Riggs,' he said hoarsely, licking his lips and wondering how long he was expected to keep his hands to himself. 'This beach barbecue.

Is it something you particularly want to go to?'

He was willing her to say no, but she shot him an amused look, her brown eyes teasing. 'It's *the* event of our pitiful social calendar, McKenna. I wouldn't miss it for the world. It's my only chance to go out.'

Which meant that she was going to make him wait.

His eyes were fastened on the dress. It looked simple enough. So why did it cling and hug and skim so cleverly? 'I'm not sure you should be going out dressed like that.'

'Well, I wouldn't normally.' She paused to fiddle with the tiny strap of the dress. 'But someone told me that I should be more impulsive so I thought I'd give it a go. And you have to record a piece to camera, if I recall, all about responsible partying and safe sex.'

Sam ran a hand over his face and tried to think about suitably sober situations. And freezing cold showers. Anything to try and subdue his reactions, which were rapidly spiralling out of control.

'Polly is waiting on the beach for you.' She walked towards the steps, the smooth swing of her hips drawing his eye. 'Let's move.'

Sam swallowed and hoped they were planning to film him from the waist up. Otherwise he was in trouble.

'Cut.' Polly walked over to Sam, ignoring the crowd that was gathering around them. It was dark on the beach, a large bonfire was blazing and the barbecue was sending out the most tempting smells imaginable, and still people just wanted to watch the filming. 'Are you all right? It's not like you to fluff it.'

Sam ran a hand through his hair, his eyes on Anna. 'Must be the audience. I'm finding them distracting.'

Polly glanced at the crowd and then back at him, puzzled. 'You're used to being stared at. Whenever we film in public, you're stared at. I don't see what's different tonight.'

'Don't you?' Sam's voice was soft and Anna felt a shiver of awareness run through her and wondered why no one else could feel the tension between them.

From the moment they'd arrived on the beach they'd been surrounded by people, Sam by the film crew and herself by local people keen to catch up and enjoy a chat. But even when they'd been separated by others, she'd sensed him watching her every move. Counting the minutes. They both knew exactly what was going to happen later and the anticipation was reaching screaming pitch.

She was starting to wonder how she was going to make it through the evening and, judging from the number of times Sam had already fluffed his piece to camera, his concentration wasn't up to much either.

Polly glanced at the cameraman. 'We've probably got enough—it's an informal setting anyway, so he doesn't have to be word perfect. We just want to give the viewer the impression that they're at a beach party—a bit of scene setting. Have we covered everything?' She checked her notes. 'Drinking, drugs, safe sex—looks about it.' She looked at the sound man. 'Are you happy?'

'Ecstatic,' he said dryly, 'and longing for a drink.'

Polly grinned. 'OK, then, folks, let's join the party.'

Sam undid his microphone and handed it back to the sound man, his eyes never leaving Anna.

She felt her heart kick against her chest as he approached. 'Hi, there.' Her voice sounded croaky, totally unlike her own. 'Are you done?'

His eyes roved over her face. 'Riggs, I haven't even begun.'

Since when had it been so difficult to breathe? Still, she couldn't resist teasing him. 'You seemed to be having one or two problems remembering your lines, McKenna.'

'My mind was elsewhere.'

Without touching, they feasted on each other, using only their eyes and the power of the mind.

Her whole body was on fire. 'You're staring, McKenna.'

'You chose to wear hot pink.'

It was foreplay, each of them knowing exactly how the encounter would end and, the anticipation heightened the excitement to almost intolerable levels.

'We're supposed to mingle, McKenna.'

His eyes dropped to her mouth. 'Really?'

'It's part of the responsibility of being a local GP,' she said huskily, longing to lift herself on tiptoe so that he could kiss her the way only he knew how. 'You have to chat to everyone.'

'Problem is, Riggs...' his gaze didn't shift from her mouth '...there's only one person here that I'm interested in.'

Heat spread through her pelvis. 'We shouldn't be seen together. It will fuel gossip.'

'I don't give a damn what other people think.'

'Easy for you to say. At the end of the summer you'll be gone and I'll be the one who's still here.'

Finally his eyes lifted back to hers. 'All right. Let's mingle.' Without another word he turned away, leaving her feeling oddly deflated and not understanding the reason. She'd been the one who'd suggested that they mingle. So why was she now disappointed that he was doing just that?

Because she wanted this whole evening to be over. She wanted this thing with Sam to start.

In the distance she saw Glenda arm in arm with one of the crew of the lifeboat and she wondered if this was the 'friend' she'd been talking about. Probably. And she was very pleased for her.

Anna moved among the crowd, chatting, laughing and all the time watching Sam out of the corner of her eye. She watched the way women crowded round him, watched the way they flirted and the way he subtly withdrew from their attentions.

Anna tightened her hand on her glass and felt her heart pound.

She decided that there was nothing quite like the adrenaline rush of knowing that, for tonight at least, Sam McKenna was hers.

He came for her at midnight.

He strolled across the sand, his shirt open at the neck, his feet bare. He looked danger-ously handsome and more temptation than a woman should have to resist.

And she had no intention of resisting him.

'We can play this two ways, Riggs,' he said conversationally, coming to a halt just inches away from her. 'We can leave right away and hope we make it back to the house, or I can just throw you down in the sand and have my wicked way with you here. Your choice.'

She caught the glitter in his blue eyes and her breath caught in her throat. 'I've never been particularly into public displays,' she murmured softly and he inclined his head and removed the plastic cup from her hand.

'In that case, we'd better go now. While we still can.' He tossed the cup into the nearest convenient bin and they strolled back along the beach towards the house.

Within minutes the music and laughter had faded into the darkness behind them and all they could hear was the hiss of the sea as it touched the sand.

They walked side by side, both barefoot, the atmosphere choked with the heavy throb of anticipation. Neither of them spoke.

When they finally reached the foot of the steps, Sam paused to let her go first.

She hesitated, suddenly filled with a nervousness that she couldn't explain. 'Sam…'

His gaze locked on hers, his eyes burning. 'I want you. Let's go to bed.'

For a moment she faltered.

Whatever they shared wouldn't last. She knew it couldn't last. They clashed too violently, they both wanted their own way too badly. They were both too strong to be a good match.

But for now…

She swallowed and then turned and sprinted up the stairs, the knowledge that he was right behind her sending her pulse skyward.

They let themselves into the house and locked the door, and she was just going to suggest that they have a drink first when he took control.

His mouth was firm, possessive and she closed her eyes and gave a whimper of pleasure, acknowledging how much of the evening she'd spent longing for his kiss.

'Much as I love the hot pink dress…' his strong hands slid the straps down her arms '…it's going to have to come off, Riggs.'

The feel of his fingers on her bare flesh made her shiver. 'Maybe we should go upstairs.' Her head tilted back and her eyes closed as he kissed his way down her neck.

'Never make it that far.'

She felt the zip go on her dress and hot pink silk pooled at her feet. 'Sam...'

He swept her up in his arms and carried her to the glass-fronted living room, refusing to let her finish her sentence. 'Let yourself go, Anna.'

And she did.

She felt herself heat and melt under the touch of his hands, for once in her life relishing the fact that someone else was taking charge.

He laid her on the thick rug, his powerful body over hers, his hands peeling away her skimpy underwear with an impatience that made her gasp.

Her fingers fumbled with the buttons of his shirt but her hands were shaking too much to complete the task and she muttered something incoherent and yanked at the fabric, sending buttons flying.

His mouth was greedy on hers and he moved his shoulders and freed himself of his shirt, his breathing ragged as his hair-roughened chest made contact with the soft mounds of her breasts. The rest of his clothes followed and their bodies tangled and locked as they moved with an erotic desperation driven by a torment of need.

And then he drove himself into her. Hard and fast, he gave them what they both needed, any notion of control abandoned from the moment they'd entered the house. Dazed and desperate, she wrapped her legs around his slick skin and moved with him, wild excitement consuming every inch of her as he hurled her to the outer reaches of pleasure. She cried out and curled her nails into his back, held on and closed her eyes as she hurtled skyward in an orgasm so intense that for a moment she lost all grip on reality.

'Anna...' He said her name harshly, fisted his hand in her hair, and her eyes flew open and locked with his. And then she felt him shudder, saw the sweat sheen on his brow and felt the hot pulse of his own release as his body pumped into hers.

She lay under him without speaking, wishing they could stay like that for ever, locked together, breathless and slick with their own passion.

Eventually he raised himself off her just enough to speak. 'Sorry.' His voice was hoarse. 'I think I forgot the foreplay.'

She chuckled, loving the weight of him on top of her. He had an amazing body. He was an amazing lover. 'I think the last few weeks have been nothing but foreplay.'

'You could have a point.'

'I hope the cameras weren't running, Dr McKenna.' She stretched underneath him, lazy and satisfied as a cat. 'You just gave a very interesting lecture to the general public on the dangers of getting carried away after parties. Of not using contraception.'

He stilled. 'Oops.'

'Yes, oops,' she agreed softly, her hand sliding over his back. 'Don't worry. I'm safe. Let's just hope none of the teenagers out there were watching your performance.'

He gave a lazy grin and touched his mouth to hers, his voice husky. 'Something wrong with my performance, Riggs?'

'I'm not sure.' She was breathless. 'I might need to evaluate it a second time. And maybe a third…'

He lifted his head further still and his lips brushed hers. Her response was instantaneous and she felt his body come alive inside her as the kiss intensified.

'I love your body.' His tongue licked into the corners of her mouth and then he withdrew from her and slid lower, breathing heat and fire over her burning skin, exploring and tasting until his mouth hovered over one nipple.

She felt the warmth of his breath and arched towards him but he held himself slightly away from her, feasting with smouldering eyes, his fingers sliding down the smooth skin of her thigh.

After the frantic, wild lovemaking session that they'd both enjoyed, this time he was taking his time.

'Sam…' She couldn't breathe, needed him so badly that every feminine part of her ached. 'Sam, please…'

His tongue flickered over her nipple and she cried out, pressing closer, her whole body quivering and shifting beneath his lean, powerful frame. Her hand slid over the bunched muscle of his shoulders and she wondered how it was possible to still want him so desperately when the most intimate part of her body still throbbed from the force of his possession.

It was impossible not to keep touching him as he was touching her, and she slid her fingers through his dark hair, loving the silkiness, the softness of it. The contrast to the hard masculinity of his body. She kissed his neck, his shoulder. Cried out as she felt his fingers touch her intimately.

She didn't understand the hunger inside her, the burning fire that didn't seem to want to be quenched. Her fingers curled round the heat of his arousal and she heard his groan, felt his body shift in response to her touch.

'Are you all right here?' His voice was gruff. 'Do you want to go upstairs?'

She slid one thigh over his. 'I'm not capable of moving.'

'Good point.' He lowered his mouth to hers. 'We'll just stay here, then. You drive me wild, Riggs. Crazy.'

'McKenna.' She slid her other thigh over his and arched against him. 'Can you stop talking and do something about the way I'm feeling?'

His chuckle was low and sexy. 'It will be my pleasure.'

CHAPTER NINE

ANNA beamed at the woman sitting across from her. 'It's so good to see you, Hilda. What can I do for you?'

Hilda looked at her curiously. 'I just wanted to ask you about this bite on my leg. It doesn't seem to want to heal.'

'Then let's take a look at it.' Anna stood up and walked round her desk, her step light. 'How long have you had it?'

'A few weeks. But it's getting worse.' Hilda stuck out the offending limb, allowing Anna to examine the calf. 'You look well, Dr Riggs. A lot more relaxed than when I last saw you.'

'I'm feeling great, Hilda.' Anna frowned at the leg. 'I don't think this is a bite. I think it's probably a flare-up of your eczema. Have you been scratching it?'

253

'Eczema?' Hilda stared down at her leg in surprise. 'Well, yes, I have been scratching it. It's been driving me mad. I assumed it was a bite.'

'Have you been very stressed?'

'It's the summer,' Hilda reminded her dryly, watching as she walked to the sink and washed her hands, 'it's my busiest time. There's a queue outside my door in the morning when I open and it stays there until I close and my counters are stripped bare of food. It's like exposing yourself to an attack of locusts. I've never known people eat so much.'

Anna laughed and sat back down at her desk. 'Well, I think that the locusts have made your eczema worse.' She tapped the keyboard. 'I'm giving you a prescription for cream to rub in that patch, and make sure you keep up your emollient baths.'

Hilda sighed. 'I'm so tired by the end of the day that if I stepped into a bath I'd probably drown.'

'It will relax you.' Anna handed her the prescription and Hilda pulled a face.

'I daren't relax. If I relax, who's going to cook for tomorrow? I just need to keep this up until the end of the summer. It isn't long now.'

Not long now.

The happiness left Anna like air from a popped balloon.

Once summer ended the tourists would be gone. And so would Sam.

The past two weeks had been idyllic. At work they were very discreet, communicating on a totally professional level, but the moment they stepped through the doors of the house they were lovers. Crazy, wild, self-absorbed lovers. And up until now she'd been so totally caught up in the madness of the present that she hadn't allowed herself to think about the future.

But the future was on her doorstep.

'You and Dr McKenna have done a good job here this summer,' Hilda said, taking the prescription and tucking it safely in her bag.

'Been just what the village needed. It was time for young blood in the practice and Sam's just the man.'

'Sam's just temporary,' Anna said briskly, reaching for some papers on her desk and trying to ignore the sick feeling in the pit of her stomach. 'He was only ever temporary.'

Only somehow, over the past few weeks, she'd allowed herself to forget that. She'd lived so much for the moment that she hadn't realised that tomorrow had arrived.

Hilda looked at her. 'He's a local lad. This is his home and this is where he should be. You know it and I know it.' She sniffed and rose to her feet, her bag clasped in her hand. 'And sooner or later Sam McKenna will work that out, too. He wanted to spread his wings and he's done that. It's time for him to stop messing around. If you want to drop by later, I've got the most delicious seafood lasagne. I'll put a couple of portions aside for you. And a lemon tart.'

'Thanks, Hilda. Without you I would undoubtedly starve.' Anna stood up and walked to the door with her. 'I'll pop by on my way home.'

She watched Hilda go and then closed the door firmly.

In a daze, she walked back to her desk and sank into her chair.

How could it have happened?

How could she have been so stupid?

She'd fallen in love with Sam. Completely and utterly.

And it wasn't supposed to be that way. They didn't like each other. They clashed terribly. They disagreed on everything. They…

She ran a hand over her face and groaned. *They were perfect together.*

So now what?

She stared out of the window, across the harbour to the estuary and the sea beyond. Hilda was wrong about Sam. He wouldn't be staying. Not once the summer was over. They hadn't talked about it yet, but both of them knew he'd be going soon. Back to his life in London.

And she couldn't blame him for that. He'd never pretended that their relationship was anything other than physical. It was her that had broken the rules. Broken the rules by falling in love.

So now what did she do? She obviously couldn't ever tell him, so what did she do? Did she end it?

She watched the boats bobbing in the harbour, the wind catching the flags on the masts, and knew that she couldn't do that.

She wanted to make the most of every minute.

She'd enjoy the relationship until it was time for him to move on.

And then she'd let him go without ever telling him how she really felt.

And spend the rest of her life trying to get over him.

He was going to tell her.

Sam stowed the surfboard in the outhouse and locked the door. Tonight he was going to tell Anna that he was in love with her.

He was convinced she felt something, too. She had to.

Feeling nervous for the first time in his thirty-two years, he showered and changed and then strolled into the kitchen. It had become their routine. He cooked for both of them, sometimes from scratch, sometimes just reheating a delicacy from Hilda's kitchen.

He opened the fridge and found a seafood lasagne. 'Thank you, Hilda,' he murmured, sliding it into the oven and then grabbing a beer from the fridge.

He could see Anna already sitting on the deck, her slim brown legs stretched in front of her, a medical journal open on her lap. She had a glass in her hand and her mobile phone was on the table in front of her.

He felt something shift inside him.

Who would have thought it?

Who would ever have thought that the two of them would develop this amazing connection?

He walked out onto the deck and bent to kiss her mouth. He couldn't resist it. All day he ached to do just that and had to hold himself in check. He didn't see why he should have to when they were at home.

She pulled away from him, dropped the medical journal and reached for her glass. 'You're late. Problems?'

'Just enjoying the surf.' He smiled and sprawled in a chair next to her. 'How was your day?'

'Fine.' She shot him a bright smile and Sam frowned slightly, sensing that something was wrong. She was different tonight. Brittle.

'Has something happened?'

Her eyes flew to his, startled. 'What could have happened?'

He was now convinced that something had. 'I don't know.' He kept his voice casual. 'It's just that you're a little jumpy.'

Her eyes slid away from his. 'I'm fine. Just hungry, I expect.'

She was lying.

Sam watched her for a minute and then rose to his feet. 'All right—let's eat.' If she was using hunger as an excuse, he'd get rid of that and then see what happened.

He served the lasagne, handed her a bowl of salad and topped up her wine.

'Eat.'

She picked up her fork and poked at the food. 'Thanks. Looks good. Hilda was in today, having trouble with her eczema. All those tourists are stressing her out.' She chattered away, always keeping the subject neutral, always avoiding eye contact.

And she hardly touched her food. She moved it around her plate, shifted its position and worried it with her fork. But hardly any made it to her mouth.

Sam started to eat. 'This is fantastic. I tell you, if she wasn't already married, I'd marry Hilda.' He loaded his fork. 'The woman is a magician in the kitchen.'

Anna put her fork down with a clatter and Sam paused, wondering what he'd said to upset her.

He frowned. If he'd upset her, he wished she'd just yell at him. At least he'd know where he stood then. 'You're not eating. What's wrong?' He reached across the table and took her hand.

She jerked it away and Sam let out a breath. 'Are you tired?'

They'd been up for most of the night making love so he wouldn't blame her if she was tired.

She chewed her lip and for a moment he thought she looked…stricken? He frowned. Why would she look stricken? 'Has something happened? Have you had bad news?'

'A bit.' She gave him a smile but it wasn't very convincing. 'Your dad called me this afternoon.'

'And?'

'And you were right. He's decided to retire. He's going to ring you, obviously, but he said as I was his partner, he owed it to me to tell me first. They're going to spend their winters in Switzerland and their summers here.' She picked up the fork and then gave up the pretence of eating and put it straight down again. 'As I said, you were right.'

Sam struggled with disappointment. For a wild moment he'd kidded himself that she looked so down because she was in love with him and trying to work out how to tell him. Clearly he couldn't have been more wrong. She was worrying about her work. Her future.

Deflated, he suddenly felt angry. He wanted her to suffer as he was suffering and clearly she wasn't. He scowled. 'You knew that would happen.'

She looked at him, startled, and he realised that his tone had probably been a little too sharp in the circumstances, but he was chewed up inside and she hadn't even *noticed*.

'Now you're the one in the funny mood.' She tilted her head to one side and studied him and he shifted uncomfortably.

Would she see? Was it written all over his face?

He didn't dare risk it. He didn't know if he could hide his feelings because he'd never had those feelings for anyone before, let alone had to hide them.

He stood up. 'I'll get pudding.'

She stared at the heaped plates. 'We haven't finished the lasagne.'

'Do you want more?'

She shook her head. 'No. I don't feel like it. Perhaps it's just too hot to eat.'

'I'll make coffee.'

He clattered around in the kitchen, venting his temper on the plates. She hadn't even mentioned him leaving. It obviously didn't bother her at all.

The irony of the situation wasn't lost on him.

How many times had he had relationships which he'd ended without a second thought, knowing that the woman in question was becoming too involved? And now here he was in that very same situation himself. He was in love with a woman who had no interest in a relationship with him. She was thinking about the practice.

'I've been thinking.' She stood in the doorway, her white strap top showing smooth brown arms and a tempting amount of cleavage. 'Would you help me interview for the new partner?'

He dropped the plate he was holding. 'Sorry. Clumsy.' He stooped and carefully picked up the shattered remains of the plate.

'It's just that you'll be going soon,' she said casually, still leaning against the doorframe, 'and I want to get a new partner as soon as possible.'

Of course she did. Anna the planner.

She couldn't wait to get rid of him.

He dropped the pieces into the bin and looked at her, his face blank of expression. 'If you place the advert, I'll help you interview.'

She smiled brightly. 'Great. We need to choose really carefully. Make sure the person is going to be happy living in such a small community. Probably have to be someone who loves the sea.'

Sam felt as though she'd punched him.

She didn't want him.

Fine.

He'd just have to learn to live without her.

She didn't know what was the matter with Sam but he was permanently in a foul mood.

And she was gutted that he hadn't offered to stay when she'd talked about interviewing a partner.

Which was utterly ridiculous, she told herself firmly, because she'd always known that he wouldn't stay. His life was in London. Why should he change his whole life just because of a little hot sex? She should have known better.

She sifted through the applications, disappointed that there were so many good doctors interested in joining her in the practice. If there'd been no one, Sam would have been forced to stay.

No, he wouldn't, she told herself crossly, he just would have found her another locum.

His new series was due to start filming in London at the end of September and she knew that he and Polly had already had several meetings about the content of the series. There was no question of him staying.

'This guy's perfect. He interviewed the best and he has all the right experience.'

'He'll leave after five minutes.'

She looked at him in exasperation. 'What is going on, McKenna? We've had a really high quality of applicants. Fantastic doctors. And you've rejected the lot of them.'

Sam toyed with his pen, a dangerous look in his eyes. 'This was my father's practice. I care about who takes it over.'

'But you don't care enough to do the job yourself,' Anna snapped, and then caught herself. She'd been trying not to quarrel with him. 'All right. What's wrong with this guy?'

The gleam in Sam's eye intensified. 'I didn't like him.'

'Well, I liked him a lot.'

For some reason that seemed to anger him even more. 'Your judgement is faulty.'

'OK, I've just about had enough of this!' She put her hands on her hips and glared at him. 'What the hell is wrong with you?'

He glared back. 'Nothing's wrong with me.'

'That's rubbish.' Temper blurred her vision. 'Whatever I do, you yell at me! You're crabby and irritable and generally bad-tempered.'

He scowled at her. 'I am not bad-tempered.'

'I haven't heard you laugh for days and we clash on everything.'

'So what's new about that? We've always clashed on everything.'

'Not since—' She broke off and swept her hair away from her face, her colour high. Their physical relationship was something that they just didn't talk about.

'Since we made the stupid mistake of sleeping together? Well, you were right about that.' He gave a crooked smile. 'It changed everything.'

Her heart skipped a beat. 'So is that why you don't come near me any more? Because it was such a stupid mistake?'

To her utter mortification she burst into tears and Sam cursed fluently.

'OK, stop that, Riggs. Don't cry.' He lifted his hands and for a moment she thought he was going to touch her for the first time in days. Then his hands dropped to his sides again and a muscle worked in his jaw. 'I can't stand it when you cry. That's a low trick. It's a girly trick and you don't do girly stuff.'

She didn't need reminding of that.

If she did more 'girly stuff' then he probably wouldn't be leaving.

Anger and frustration burst free inside her. 'I'm crying because I hate you. I hate you, McKenna.' She sniffed loudly and scrubbed the tears away with the back of her hand. 'I really hate you for making me feel this way.'

His hands were still by his sides but she noticed that his fists were clenched. 'What way?'

'Angry.' She blew her nose hard. 'And—and—as if I could strangle you with my bare hands. And sad.' Her eyes filled again. 'You make me sad.'

He was looking at her in horror. 'Sad?'

'Yes, sad. Because what we had was good and it couldn't last.' She blinked and sniffed again. 'Oh, damn. This is all so stupid. It's fine. I'm fine. The sooner you go, the better. At least I get to run this practice in peace, without your input. Your ideas never work anyway, McKenna. You're always wrong.'

'I'm never wrong.' He frowned and raked long fingers through his hair. 'And my ideas always work. Which one didn't work? Name one that didn't work.'

She dropped the tissue in the bin and swallowed, back in control. She could do this. She could watch him walk away and she could carry on her life without him. 'Well, the teenage clinic, for one. We've got the entire village youth congregating here every Friday. It's a nightmare.'

He folded his arms across his chest and looked smug. 'So, in other words, I was right and you were wrong. I said people would come.'

'You were not right. Half of them don't even bother talking to the doctor or the practice nurse. We're not supposed to be running a youth club.'

'But they have the chance to talk to someone if they want to. And don't underestimate the power of peer pressure. If a few of them are talking to the doctor, the others will. Admit it. I was right.'

'They'll stop coming as soon as winter sets in.'

'They won't stop coming.'

She glared at him again. 'Well, you don't care anyway. You won't be here to see it. You'll be back in your fancy television studio, advising people on ingrowing toenails.' Except that wasn't what he did. She knew

272 THE CELEBRITY DOCTOR'S PROPOSAL

that now. 'I'm going to ring that guy, that Dr Hampton, and offer him the job.'

'I'll do it.' He held out his hand and took the details from her. 'That way I can co-ordinate dates with him.'

She felt the tears start again and bit them back. 'Fine. Just as long as someone is here to do the work.'

'Fine. I'll arrange it.'

Sam stared at the details of the doctor.

Anna liked him.

The thought made him want to smash his fist into something.

And he was about to offer him the job. Once he picked up that phone, this guy would become a GP in a village practice. He would surf in the evenings and at the weekends, he'd eat Hilda's beautiful seafood dishes and lemon tart and he'd join the lifeboat crew for drinks on the quay. He'd walk the cliffs, run on the sand and sail yachts. But most of all he'd work alongside Anna. They'd make decisions together, develop the practice to-gether, plan for their patients.

Would they sleep together?

Sam's fingers tightened on the pen he was holding and he reached for the phone.

He'd better get it over with.

'There's a trailer for Sam's new series this afternoon. I've set the TV and video in the coffee-room,' Glenda said happily as Anna handed her a pile of forms. 'He and Polly have been thick as thieves all day.'

Anna gritted her teeth.

She shouldn't mind. It shouldn't matter to her. She and Sam were over.

'Have you heard anything from Dr Hampton?' She was surprised that he hadn't been in touch with her. It was all very well for Sam to have confirmed all the details, but surely the man would still want to contact her?

'A letter came this morning.' Glenda handed it over, oddly hesitant.

Anna scanned it, blinked, scanned it again and then her temper exploded. 'Where is he?'

Glenda flinched. 'If you mean Dr McKenna, he's just parked his car and he's walking through the doors as we speak. But, Anna—'

Anna whirled round, lights flashing in her brain as she came face to face with him. 'Of all the miserable, vile, small-minded b—'

'We've got an audience, Riggs,' Sam interrupted her, an answering flash of anger in his blue eyes as he faced her head on. 'You might want to hold onto that temper of yours.'

'I don't care who hears this.' She tossed her hair back, her gaze furious as she waved the letter under his nose. 'You were supposed to offer him the job, McKenna. You were supposed to tell him that he was the one.'

'He wasn't the one.' Sam tried to step past her, a muscle flickering in his jaw. 'I didn't think he was the right person for the job.'

'Well, I did!'

He turned on her. 'I'm well aware of that.' He growled the words like a man goaded to the extremes of his tolerance. 'You made it perfectly clear how much you liked him.'

'And what's wrong with that?' She spread her hands in a gesture of disbelief. 'I was going to work with the guy. I was *supposed* to like him. Or is that what this is all about?' Her hands fell to her sides and she glared at him. 'Is it jealousy, McKenna? Is that's what's wrong?'

They were both breathing rapidly, eyes locked in combat, totally indifferent to their growing audience.

Polly cleared her throat. 'Sam, your new trailer is on air in about two minutes. Why don't we all watch it?'

Sam sucked in a breath, his eyes still on Anna's. 'Fine. Let's watch it.'

Anna had to stop herself from screaming. She didn't want to watch his trailer. She didn't want to see what his plans for the future were because she knew they didn't involve her and that knowledge made her want to cry like a baby.

She stuck her chin in the air. 'Fine. Let's watch the trailer.'

She stalked into the staffroom where Glenda was already glued to the screen. 'Here we go…'

'This autumn, *Medical Matters* moves from London to the seaside, following the trials and tribulations of life in a busy harbour practice…'

The narrator's voice droned on and then there was Sam, standing on the beach, his dark hair blowing in the wind as he talked.

When he'd finished, Glenda pressed the 'pause' button and stared at Anna.

Anna stood in silence.

She opened her mouth to speak and then closed it again.

Sam's eyes were fixed on her face. 'Say something.'

She swallowed. 'You're going to make the programme here?'

Polly grinned. 'It was that or he was going to resign, and I'm not about to lose my best medical presenter.'

Anna stared at him. 'You were going to resign?' She stared at the TV. 'It said this autumn.'

'The trailer is for you, Riggs,' Sam said roughly. 'We made it just for you. The real series and trailer won't be shown until next summer.'

Her expression was blank. 'Sorry?'

He glared at her in exasperation. 'It's a message from me to you,' he shouted, 'but you're so damn stupid you can't even see it!'

'If you stopped yelling, maybe I'd be able to concentrate,' Anna yelled, lifting a hand to her chest. Suddenly it was difficult to breathe. 'I don't understand.'

'I didn't give the guy the job because I decided that I wanted it myself!' Sam paced the room, his hands thrust in his pockets, his eyes stormy. 'I decided that everything he was gaining I was losing, and I discovered that I didn't want to lose it.' He stopped pacing and looked at her. 'I discovered that I wanted it for myself.'

Anna went still. 'What did you want for yourself?'

'The practice.' He ran a hand over the back of his neck and swore softly. 'And you. I wanted you. Which makes me an idiot, I know, because you've made it perfectly obvious that you don't want me.'

He wanted her?

Anna struggled to speak. 'Hold on.' Her voice was scratchy. 'When did I make it perfectly obvious that I didn't want you? When?'

He shrugged. 'When you started advertising for new partners.'

'I was forced to look for another partner because you were leaving, McKenna!'

'I never said I was leaving.'

'Well, you never said you might stay.' She lifted a shaking hand to her hair and scooped it back. 'And—and you stopped sleeping with me.'

'Because you'd clearly planned your life without me.'

'Because that was how you wanted it!'

They were both shouting, emotions running high, oblivious to the fact that they had an audience. A highly entertained audience. Polly glanced at Glenda.

'Time for us to leave, I think,' she muttered, and Glenda grinned.

'Can we listen at the door?'

They slipped out of the room, unnoticed.

'Why would I have wanted it?' He paced the floor again. 'What we had was amazing. I've never had that with anyone before.'

Her heart jammed in her throat. 'I'm not your sort of woman.'

'What's that supposed to mean?'

'You don't want me. I'm not girly and I can't cook.'

'I don't give a damn whether you can cook.' He frowned, confused. 'I can cook perfectly well myself and if I can't be bothered then Hilda's always standing in the wings. I don't see what your lack of skills in the kitchen has got to do with our relationship.'

'You want a traditional woman. I'm not who you want.'

'Damn it, Riggs! Haven't you heard a single word I've said?' He strode towards her and grabbed her by the arms, shaking her slightly. 'You are exactly who I want. I love you. I want to be with you. I know you don't love me back, but I can still be a decent partner in the practice.'

'You love me?'

His hands dropped. 'That's what I said.'

'Why didn't you say that you loved me before now?'

'Because I'm not some sort of masochist, and you made it perfectly clear that my feelings aren't returned. That I'm not your type—or in your plans.'

Anna shook her head, feeling slightly dizzy. 'They are returned. I love you, too.'

'You stride around here making plans for my replacement while I'm still in your bed, and you—' He broke off and stared at her.

'What did you say? That last thing—what did you say?'

'I said I love you.' She tried hard to breathe normally. 'And if I talked about your replacement, it was only because you never once mentioned the fact that you were tempted to stay on.'

He was still staring. 'I don't think we've been communicating very well.'

'Possibly not.'

'We're probably going to have to work on that.'

'Probably.'

He slid a hand into his pocket. 'This partnership. Are you willing to make it permanent?'

She stared at the box in his hand. 'Is that what I think it is?'

'Yes.' He opened the box and lifted the ring out.

She gasped and covered her mouth with her hand. 'It's stunning.'

He took her hand. 'Will you marry me?'

She blinked back tears as he slid the ring onto her finger. 'If you're willing to risk the fact that I might poison you in the kitchen.'

'You won't be allowed in the kitchen.' His voice was hoarse as he hauled her against him and bent his head to hers. 'There are other rooms in the house that are going to take priority.'

Some considerable time later Anna pulled away, her heart thumping. 'You do realise that your parents are going to be horribly smug about all this,' she muttered against his mouth. 'They'll think it's because of them.'

'I never do anything my parents want,' Sam reminded her, his eyes still half shut as he studied her face. 'If we're together, it's in spite of them.'

'Your mum will be knitting like mad.'

He brushed his mouth against hers. 'Good. Given the number of pregnancies that happen in this village, I'd say that was sensible planning.'

She giggled and kissed him back. 'I love you. Even if you are sometimes wrong about things.'

'I love you, too.' The corner of his mouth lifted and his eyes gleamed. 'And I'm never wrong about anything.'

'You drive me nuts, McKenna.'

'Always have done, always will do.' And he lowered his mouth to hers.

MEDICAL ROMANCE™

Large Print

Titles for the next six months...

February

HOLDING OUT FOR A HERO	Caroline Anderson
HIS UNEXPECTED CHILD	Josie Metcalfe
A FAMILY WORTH WAITING FOR	Margaret Barker
WHERE THE HEART IS	Kate Hardy

March

THE ITALIAN SURGEON	Meredith Webber
A NURSE'S SEARCH AND RESCUE	Alison Roberts
THE DOCTOR'S SECRET SON	Laura MacDonald
THE FOREVER ASSIGNMENT	Jennifer Taylor

April

BRIDE BY ACCIDENT	Marion Lennox
COMING HOME TO KATOOMBA	Lucy Clark
THE CONSULTANT'S SPECIAL RESCUE	Joanna Neil
THE HEROIC SURGEON	Olivia Gates

MILLS & BOON®

Live the emotion

0106 LP 2P P1 Medical

MEDICAL ROMANCE™

Large Print

May

THE NURSE'S CHRISTMAS WISH — Sarah Morgan
THE CONSULTANT'S CHRISTMAS PROPOSAL
— Kate Hardy
NURSE IN A MILLION — Jennifer Taylor
A CHILD TO CALL HER OWN — Gill Sanderson

June

GIFT OF A FAMILY — Sarah Morgan
CHRISTMAS ON THE CHILDREN'S WARD — Carol Marinelli
THE LIFE SAVER — Lilian Darcy
THE NOBLE DOCTOR — Gill Sanderson

July

HER CELEBRITY SURGEON — Kate Hardy
COMING BACK FOR HIS BRIDE — Abigail Gordon
THE NURSE'S SECRET SON — Amy Andrews
THE SURGEON'S RESCUE MISSION — Dianne Drake

MILLS & BOON®

Live the emotion

0106 LP 2P P2 Medical

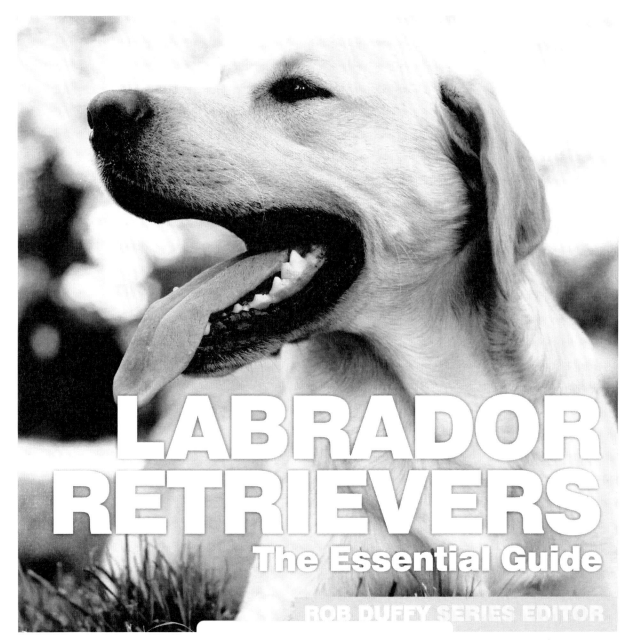

LABRADOR
RETRIEVERS
The Essential Guide

ROB DUFFY SERIES EDITOR

014314379 1

Published in Great Britain in 2019 by
need2know
Remus House
Coltsfoot Drive
Peterborough
PE2 9BF
Telephone 01733 898103
www.need2knowbooks.co.uk
All Rights Reserved
© Need2Know
SB ISBN 978-1-91084-341-3
Cover photograph: Adobe Stock